# QUICK TRICK

ROUGH RIDERS HOCKEY SERIES

SKYE JORDAN

This book is a work of fiction. References to real people, events, establishments, organizations, or locations are intended only to provide a sense of authenticity, and are used fictitiously. All other characters, and all incidents and dialogue, are drawn from the author's imagination and are not to be construed as real.

against one of the double glass doors again, then blew into his palm to warm it and raised his voice to yell, "Hello?"

No movement. No sound. Nothing.

Grant pulled out his phone and checked the time. One minute after six p.m. They'd closed early. Typical.

"Damn hick town."

He shoved his phone back into the pocket of his jacket and his hand back into his glove, then turned and looked both directions down Main Street. It was deserted on this bitterly cold night just a couple of weeks before Christmas. Not much had changed about the storybook setting—one that belonged at Santa's workshop in the North Pole. But Grant had been gone long enough for the sugary-sweet gingerbread on every building to make him gag a little. And he was sure Holly dominated ninety percent of North Carolina's power grid from Halloween through New Year's with all the additional lights and moving decorations residents added for the holidays. As if they needed more.

Across the street, a lone human figure dressed in a dark parka emerged from the shadowed storefronts and shuffled across the street. "Whatcha need there, son?"

That was just like this place—everyone up in everyone else's business.

The voice identified him as an older man, and as he approached the sidewalk, Grant caught a look at his face beneath the hood of his jacket, confirming he was in his sixties.

"Christmas tree," Grant said. "If I go home without it, my mama's gonna be pissed."

The man harrumphed and narrowed his eyes. "Which mama would that be?"

"Hazel Saber."

The man stopped and straightened out of the cold hunch that populated the streets of Holly this time of year. He pushed his hood back with a gloved hand. "Grant? That you?"

# 1

Grant Saber peered through the wide plate glass windows of St. Nicholas Hardware, searching the darkness for signs of life.

He cupped his gloved hands around his eyes to cut the glare from millions of Christmas lights reflecting off the snow and searched the shadows. This crazy-ass little town was dressed up for Christmas three hundred sixty-five days a year. As a kid, that had seemed fun. As a teen, it had seemed just plain stupid. As an adult... Well, he'd bailed on this place as soon as humanly possible.

And he sure as shit didn't want to be here now.

"I know you're in there, dammit." He could see a light burning somewhere in the back.

His breath created a billow of condensation, obscuring his view. He shifted from foot to foot, as if that would keep the blood from freezing in his veins. He might spend half his life on the ice, but the exertion and adrenaline of hockey always kept him dripping in sweat. Now he was just freezing his ass off.

Grant yanked off a ski glove and rapped his knuckles

The weathered face looking back at Grant flooded him with a rush of great memories. Some of the best he had of his youth here in Holly.

"Mr. Lowry?" Mike Lowry was the father of one of Grant's best friends and teammates all through school. Grant laughed and stepped forward to hug the man he spent so many years wishing had been his father rather than the man he'd been born to. "How are you?"

Mike gave him the same bear hug he'd always shared, and nostalgic warmth softened a few of Grant's rough edges. "Good, good." He stepped back with a big smile creasing his face. He'd probably aged more than a decade over the last ten years, but he still looked great to Grant. "I've been watching all your games, you know, since you went pro. Even sprung for cable so I could watch the ones on those oddball channels."

Grant laughed at the farmer's rough language and made a mental note to pay the man's cable bill into perpetuity. "That's great. How's Bobby doing?"

"Oh, real good." The freezing temperatures didn't quicken Mike's lazy drawl. "Got himself a farm of his own in Bonnettsville. Married Becky Snell 'bout four years ago. They've got a three-year-old little girl and another baby on the way. Bobby's hopin' for a boy this time. One he can take out on the ice with him."

"He can take a girl on the ice," Grant said, working to engage in the conversation. Every word reminded him of why he'd been so anxious to get out of this town. The whole stuck-on-a-farm-with-a-wife-and-kids scenario was making invisible walls close in on him.

"Aw, well, he don't get out on the ice much anymore anyway. But wait until everyone hears we've got a star in our midst this Christmas. Did I hear you're gonna be working with Dwayne and the high school team?"

"Yeah." Remembering the positive half of what had brought

him back to Holly helped smooth the frustration he'd met up with upon arriving—his mother. "I'm really looking forward to it."

"Bet he is too. Since MaryAnn passed, he's real lonely. Bends the ear of anyone who will listen. Those kids keep him going, you know? It'll be real good for him to see you."

Mike kept talking, and Grant was reminded of how many people in this town loved to bend an ear. He just kept nodding while Mike talked about Dwayne, the high school hockey team, his granddaughter, and Bobby's farm until Grant could find a spot to cut in.

"Well, say hi to Bobby for me, would you?" Grant said. "I'll be in town for a few weeks. I'd love to have a beer with him if he's around."

"Oh, he'd like that. Say, how's your shoulder? It's been keepin' you off the ice, right?"

"Yes, sir, but not for much longer. Surgery was a success, and I'm done with PT. Just waiting for the doctors to clear me. I should be back in the game after the holiday break."

And, God, he *could not wait*. He'd been going stir-crazy. There was only so much working out he could do. So many training tapes he could watch. So many soft practices he could participate in. So many wanna-be Rider Girls to coach through riding lessons.

Okay, there was an endless supply of wanna-be Rider Girls. But in truth, Grant wouldn't mind a little variety. Though he wasn't exactly in a place where variety was bursting at the seams.

"Bet your parents are glad to see you," Mike said.

Grant thought of his mother's demand to fetch the Christmas tree less than an hour after he'd arrived home and clenched his teeth. "Highly debatable," he muttered and glanced toward the store again. "And definitely not if I don't come home with a tree. They closed early."

sideline during practices, and auditioning Rider Girls, Grant needed some heavy-duty Zs.

He stepped into the bar, taking a minute to let his eyes adjust while he searched for this "prettiest little blonde in town."

The space had been upgraded over the years. Now a mahogany bar stretched along one wall, complete with antique brass footrests. Behind that, bottles of alcohol lined the mirrored wall. The seating area combined booths and tables in dark wood that gave the place that true Irish pub feel, rivaling some of the most authentic pubs Grant had visited during his travels in Boston, Philly, and Chicago.

Too bad they'd gone and fucked up a good thing with all the Christmas crap—on the walls, on the tables, art, figurines, decorations...

The only blonde who caught Grant's eye sat at the bar, chatting with a brunette woman about the same age. But this blonde was beyond pretty, and Grant instantly recognized Faith Nicholas, and not someone he'd expected to see back in Holly. She was probably visiting for the holidays, like half the other people in town.

From where he stood, she looked even prettier now than she'd been back in high school—if you liked the girl-next-door type. Grant might have been into Faith back then, but the "sweetest little thing in town" was definitely *not* what he wanted in a woman now.

Her hair was cut shoulder-length and styled straight and sleek, but that was where her sophistication ended. She sported the typical small-town country girl look with worn jeans, a thin tweedy sweater, and low-heeled, knee-high, tan suede boots. Grant had only been here an hour, and he was already missing the refinement of the city.

The sooner he got that tree for his parents, the sooner he could go to bed. The sooner he got to bed, the sooner he could hit the ice with the kids in the morning. And as the daughter of the man who owned the hardware store, Faith Nicholas would be the most likely person to know how he could find the girl running it.

He stepped forward just as a man strolled up to the bar beside Faith. He leaned his elbow on the shiny mahogany, and whatever he said drew the gazes of both women, giving Grant a better look at Faith.

With one of the bar's spotlights spilling over her, Grant got a better look at her cheekbones, the shape of her face, her smile… She was a real beauty. If she were decked out in a form-fitting dress, four-inch fuck-me heels, and a little makeup, she'd be the kind of woman Grant would have locked on to at a party. The kind he would have worked his way toward until he'd started a conversation and held her complete attention.

But they weren't in DC. And she wasn't decked out. Still, that smile of hers sure lit up a room. And even from yards away, Grant could feel its warmth seeping into his belly. She slipped off the barstool and turned toward the man who'd approached. Grant's gaze rolled down her backside.

"Damn," he muttered under his breath. "That girl rocks her jeans."

Maybe a little bit of country was just the variety he was looking for. Only, last time he'd seen Faith Nicholas, it was beside Dillon Brady. The high school football star had carried Faith on his arm all four years. They'd been slated for marriage and kids immediately after college.

Grant glanced around the bar again, this time searching for Faith's other half. But no one even resembling Brady caught Grant's eye. Nor did any other pretty blonde. He returned his gaze to Faith, but that guy was still there, trying to make headway. He was an all-around average guy. Average height, average build, average dress, average looking.

Grant glanced at his watch, crossed his arms, and leaned

against the wall. If she was still the same Faith she'd been in high school, this wouldn't take long. She'd brush off Mr. Average within minutes. She'd been the valedictorian, the head of half a dozen different clubs, the star of the swim team, the homecoming queen, and the girlfriend of the most popular guy in their class, if not the school. She'd certainly never taken a second look at Grant, who'd been as average then as the Joe chatting her up now.

While he waited, Grant glanced at Faith's left hand, surprised to find it bare.

"Wonder what happened to Mr. Football Star."

But he didn't have much time to wonder, because Average Joe had just been shot down and returned to his table, while Faith and the brunette started talking again.

"Some things never change."

But some things did. Like Grant. He'd changed three hundred percent. He might not feel the need to prove himself to the people of this town anymore, but he was going to have to turn on a little of his swagger to get her to help him out tonight.

No problem.

Nowadays, Grant had swagger to spare.

# 2

"And another one bites the dust." Faith's best friend, Taylor Sullivan, shook her head in disgust.

Faith gave Taylor her get-serious look. "He undressed my Barbies in second grade."

"*Everyone* undressed Barbies in second grade."

"Not like him. Creepy, I'm telling you."

"What's creepy is that you *remember* how he undressed your Barbies in second grade and that you *still* hold it against him." Taylor used her wineglass to point at Faith. "That's creepy. You're not looking for forever here, Faith. You're looking for a date. You're looking for casual. You're looking for a—"

Faith plugged her ears. "La-la-la-la-la."

Taylor rolled her eyes. "Nothing any guy did last month, let alone in second grade, matters right now. What matters right now is you getting a life."

"Hey, I have a life. *Plenty* of it, thank you very much. And I have the bills and headaches to prove it." Faith picked up her second glass of Jingle Jangle punch, longing to escape the stress. For a night. An hour. Hell, she'd settle for a moment at this point. "In fact, in my opinion, I have a little *too much* life."

"Too much bad and not enough good. Which is why—"

"Which is why"—Faith cut her off—"what I *really* need is more of this." She savored the delicious blend of juice, berries, vodka, and Grand Marnier, licking the sugar from the rim off her lips with a hum of pleasure. "And less of you reminding me of exactly what I don't need—more trouble."

"Why do you equate men with trouble?"

Faith laughed and focused on her friend. Taylor looked pretty tonight, just a touch of makeup brightening her eyes and cheeks, her dark hair falling in loose waves to her collarbone. She looked so young and so fresh and so happy. Happiness that came from Taylor's son, Caleb. And even though the boy also brought Faith an incredible amount of joy as her godson, she was too aware that all her own family was gone.

To Taylor's question, Faith smiled and shrugged. "Show me one person who's given me a different perspective."

Taylor's angelic face compressed in a silly frown. "You know what you need for Christmas this year?"

"I'm sure you're going to tell me."

"You need one great big O, that's what."

Taylor's declaration took Faith off guard, and she burst out laughing. She didn't disagree with Taylor. Wouldn't even argue if a man worthy of the honor came along, because the truth was, Faith could use quite a few orgasms to make up for the years without a man in her life. But the fact still remained...

"You're just trying to get out of finding dating material in this crowd," Taylor teased, "because you know you can't."

"You didn't say anything about dating material," Faith sassed back. "You said a guy who wasn't trouble, and I can too find that in this crowd." She let out a huff and glanced around the bar.

Faith did the same, laughing at their tipsy argument. Luckily, they could both walk home. In the crowd milling around the bar, Faith saw the same people she always saw in Holly, local residents. Plus a few people who had moved away and come back to visit family. A few tourists here and there, mostly older couples. A couple of kids home on college break.

Despite Taylor's belief that Faith never even entertained the idea of dating again, she did indeed think about it often. Actually, what she thought about more often than dating was just plain old sex. But even that was impossible with the mess in her life right now. Besides, she hadn't crossed paths with anyone remotely interesting who also happened to be available.

"Not all guys are trouble," Taylor insisted. "How about Tom? Tom and Mildred have been together forty-eight years. He can't be trouble if she's stayed with him through six kids and fifteen grandkids."

Faith slipped off her stool, turned from the bar, leaned back against the mahogany, and scanned the direction of Taylor's gaze. But instead of finding Tom, a retired banker in town, her gaze stumbled on a man near the door. Someone she didn't recognize. A big man in a ball cap, sliding out of a parka. She couldn't see his whole face beneath the cap's brim, but he looked young, about her age, and had a nice jawline. The body he unveiled beneath his jacket was even better, stretching his long-sleeved tee with the kind of muscle Faith hadn't seen outside television or magazines in years. The kind that made sparks tingle low in her gut. He definitely wasn't from here. She would have noticed that body in her store.

"And Adam," Taylor continued while Faith scanned the stranger from his wide chest to his snow-covered boots. "He's a great guy. So is his brother, Dale. And their cousin, Tim, who lives in the next county—"

"Is a serial cheater." Faith forced her gaze off the stranger and refocused on Taylor with a smile.

"And how would you know that?"

"Hardware store, remember? Guys forget I'm a girl. They talk to me and around me like I'm one of their buddies. And I know Tim's been off and on with Kelly for months because he keeps cheating on her. Something both Dale and Adam encourage. And even though Tim has a son by Kelly, Dale and Adam keep telling him he should leave 'the nagging bitch'"—she put the words in air quotes—"and move on. Don't try to tell me those men aren't trouble."

Taylor faced her and leaned against the bar again. "That's your problem. You know too much."

"I don't consider that a problem. I consider *not knowing* a problem."

"You never give anyone a chance, Faith."

She looked down at her drink with half her mind wondering who Sexy at the door belonged to. And wishing she could give him a chance. A big-old-O-for-Christmas chance.

"I'm not looking for trouble again. Been there, done that." She really couldn't face being left again either. But that was something she kept to herself. "What I am looking for and what I really need for Christmas is some relief from these money worries. The best thing you could do for me would be to sit your butt in a chair and tell me what you've got going on YouTube and how I can tap into that."

Taylor heaved an exhausted sigh.

When she didn't start talking, Faith said, "If you don't tell me, I'm going to ask Caleb. Do you want your eleven-year-old teaching me how to make a YouTube video? 'Cause I know he knows how."

"Don't you dare. He's already too obsessed with the computer as it is." She put her hands up in surrender. "Okay, okay. I'll talk shop on one condition."

"Oh God. What?"

"You flirt with the next guy who comes up to you."

"Flirt? No, uh-uh. I don't flirt. I've never flirted." She waved the topic away and turned the conversation back around. Taylor had developed her hobby of blogging and creating

YouTube videos into a full-fledged, lucrative career. It wasn't something Faith ever believed she'd consider doing, but right now, she was looking at all possibilities.

"I've been seriously thinking about doing a little of what you're doing with the blogging and videos, but with segments on things I know about, like hardware and fix-it projects. You know, repairing a hole in drywall, fixing a leaky faucet, that sort of thing. I've researched it online and I see them out there, but they're horrible. I could do it way better, but figuring out where to start is overwhelming. I've never talked on camera, I don't know how to target an audience, I barely even use Facebook. And I sure can't afford professional equipment."

She took a breath, set down her drink, and rubbed her temples. "Even with the increase in holiday sales, the store isn't going to keep me afloat. And if it's not keeping me afloat, it won't keep anyone afloat, which means I wouldn't be able to sell it. I need to do *something* before I lose *everything*." She lifted her gaze to Taylor and rested her chin in her hands. "So, what do you think? Are the videos worth my time?"

Taylor exhaled, but the softened look in her eyes gave Faith a little hope. "You are exasperating."

She smiled. "I'm aware."

"Yes, I think it's worth the time. There are a lot of DIY videos out there, but like you said, most of them suck. If you do it right, handle your links and sponsorships right, build a following, you could eventually make a significant income."

Relief loosened Faith's shoulders, and she turned her brightest smile on Taylor. "I don't know anything about links or sponsorships, but I really like the sound of 'significant income.' So you'll show me the ropes?"

"I'll make you a deal. You give *one guy* a chance, and I'll get you started."

Faith's expression fell. "That's blackmail. Friends don't blackmail friends."

"Excuse me, Miss Nicholas."

The man's voice rolled over her from behind. Deep, slow, confident. Without even looking, she was sure it belonged to Sexy at the door. Faith narrowed her eyes on Taylor. "Did you set this up?"

"You wish." She widened her eyes a fraction and tipped her head slightly, a gesture Faith read as *take a look.*

Frustration burned. She was a grown woman, dammit, and she could handle her own relationships—or lack thereof.

She turned—and faced Sexy. Faith could see his face beneath the cap now, and he was sinfully scrumptious in more ways than she could even sum up in the moment. Like his voice, the man exuded confidence. He had light eyes, thick dark lashes, and full lips, quirked in a half grin.

A grin that told her he also knew just how attractive he was. She'd certainly seen that look enough to know. Only wished she'd learned to identify it a lot sooner than she had. Figured the only guy who'd caught her eye in...forever...would be full of himself.

"I'm buying my own drinks tonight," she said, hoping she sounded more congenial than she felt. "And I'm not interested in going out, but thanks anyway."

Faith slid back onto her stool with a pinch of guilt in her gut. She couldn't remember the last time she'd been so rude. She was clearly too overwhelmed to even *think* about having a man in her life.

She opened her mouth to tell Taylor she was going home, but Sexy spoke first.

"Actually, I wasn't going to offer you a drink *or* ask for a date. But thanks for saving me the trouble—in the event either of those ever crossed my mind."

He had just the hint of an accent. A bizarre tang she'd never heard before—a little Carolina, a little...Jersey? Boston? Wisconsin?

Faith swiveled again, meeting the man's gaze squarely, caught between petulance and anger. He was leaning on the bar, his head turned toward her. And his grin had grown, creating crinkles at the corners of his eyes. Damn, those were pretty eyes. His hat bore the New York Mets logo, and dark hair snuck out from under the edges.

"Just a heads-up, handsome," she said. "If you decide to ask any woman out around here, you'd better ditch the hat. No self-respecting Carolina girl dates a Mets fan."

He huffed a laugh, and a real smile beamed across his face. One that made Faith's stomach twist and flip.

"That so?" he asked.

"That's so."

"Who would a self-respecting Carolina girl date?"

"Atlanta Braves fan, of course. Ask anyone."

His gaze darted to Taylor. "That right? Are you a Braves fan?"

"Hell yes," Taylor confirmed.

"Duly noted." He nodded and returned his gaze to Faith. "Miss Nicholas, if I promise not to wear my Mets hat in your presence again, would you tell me how I can find the woman running your father's hardware store?"

She lifted one brow. No one called it her father's store anymore. "Can I ask why?"

He chuckled and turned his gaze to the bar. "Well, see, my mama sent me to pick up our family Christmas tree." He turned his gaze back on her with his panty-melting charisma ramped up to full power. His eyes were hot, his voice warm. "I was at the hardware store ten minutes before close, but it was already shut down tight. We've got a tradition, a big dinner where all the kids and grandkids and nieces and nephews and cousins all get together and decorate the tree. And, I tell you, if I go home without it..." He sucked air between his teeth with a shake of his head and his gaze lowered in a slow sweep of her face to hold on her mouth. "I'm as good as skinned."

"Aw," Taylor said behind Faith, her friend's voice signaling she'd fallen for the story like a rock in a river. "How sweet."

Faith laughed and straightened to put a little more distance between her and this tricked-out version of her ex. "You can certainly spin a tale that pulls on the heartstrings, and I imagine most women fall for you hook, line, and sinker." She paused long enough for him to lift his brows in a what-can-I-say expression, then continued. "But I work with men all day, every day. Which means I can see right through bullshit. Everything you said after picking up your family Christmas tree was a big fat lie. You weren't there ten minutes early, and there's no family get-together tonight. But the part about getting skinned might be true. Otherwise, I doubt a city boy like you would be wasting your time chasing down some country bumpkin to get a Christmas tree."

His brow fell. His smile faded into an irritated smirk.

*Bingo.* She'd been guessing at about forty percent of that information, but maybe she was a better judge of character than she thought.

Faith picked up her punch, finished the drink, then licked the last bit of sugar from the rim before meeting his gaze again. "Now, why don't you start again, and try the truth this time."

He repositioned himself, facing her with an annoyed sigh. "My mama looked at the kitchen clock, realized it was five minutes till six, and rushed me out the door to get the tree before the store closed. And even though I *did* get there a few minutes before six, the store was locked up tight, so it *did* close early. And yes, the skinning part was true, which means one of two things for me."

Oh, she liked this version of the man much better. And he was more entertaining than arguing with Taylor, so she dropped her chin into her hand and indulged him. "I'm listening."

"One—you tell me how to get ahold of the girl who works the shop so I can try to sweet-talk her into letting my tree out of hock, or two..." He heaved another long-suffering sigh. "I pull a saw from my daddy's garage, hike into the wilderness in the dark, and cut one down."

Faith's brows shot up. "You're *that* afraid of your mama?"

He winced and huffed out a you-got-me chuckle. "I'm *that* afraid of my mama."

Faith broke into laughter.

Taylor pushed to her feet. "Well, I've got to get home. My babysitter's parents don't like her out too late." She leaned in to hug Faith and whispered, "*Get yourself a Christmas present, dammit*" in her ear.

When she turned to leave without even saying hello or good-bye to Sexy, Faith called after her, "Do you still need me to watch Caleb Saturday?"

"Uh, no, no," she said in a way that told Faith she was lying so Sexy would believe she was available. "You are free as a bird." And she blew a kiss before slipping into her jacket and out the front door.

Faith exhaled and faced temptation again. Sexy had that freakin' adorable lopsided grin on his face. And it was less arrogant now. More...interested?

*Pffft.*

More interested in getting his goddamned tree from the store, maybe. Guys like this weren't interested in her. Not for real. She was glad she was tipsy, or that very true realization would have stung. Especially when he stood so close, his spicy, masculine scent turned her blood to lava.

She took another drink from her Jangle punch—no point in letting good alcohol go to waste—and asked, "What city did you slide in from?"

He frowned, then looked down at himself. After a second, he met her gaze again. "There is nothing about me that says city."

She laughed, gesturing in a circle at him, and said, "All... this. Everything from that Marmot parka to those L.L.Bean boots says city boy coming home for Christmas."

He leaned back, one brow cocked. "These boots aren't from L.L.Bean."

"No?" she asked, smiling at the way he took the slight in stride.

"No. They're Cabela's."

"Ah, well, I stand corrected. I've gotta warn you, everyone only thinks the girl working the store is sweet because of all that sugar on the outside. But I know her, and I'd suggest you prepare yourself to go cut yourself a tree."

"And I have a knack with sweet talk," he said, turning on some attitude. "Why don't you point me in her direction, and we'll just see how it works out."

She chuckled and lifted her drink to finish it off. Setting it down with a clink on the lacquered wood, she said, "Don't bother. I'm the girl running the shop, and sweet talk bounces off me like bullets off Kevlar."

A mix of confusion and humor quirked his mouth again. "Bullets don't bounce off Kevlar."

"They do when you've had two glasses of Kelly's Jangle punch."

That made him laugh, and the low, rich sound of it tingled through her belly.

"But, you're in luck. I happen to be on my way home, so I'll get the tree for you." She slid off the stool, and her legs brushed his. He made no move to pull back, and Faith had just enough liquid courage in her to stand her ground and meet his gaze directly. "But here's the deal, handsome, and there will be no negotiation. I'll open up long enough for you to pick up the tree, period. There will be no other transactions. No stand, no ornaments, no tinsel. You're getting nothing but the tree. Are we clear?"

He tipped his head. "I don't know, that tinsel, that could be a deal breaker."

"Smart-ass." She pointed a finger at his head. "And no Mets hat."

He rolled his eyes but swiped it off his head, stashed it behind his back, and grinned.

His hair was black, cut short, but growing out of the style and curling at the edges. His teeth were straight and bright. His cheeks were dotted with two shallow dimples.

Damn, he was *adorable*. Her heart tripped.

"Better?" he asked.

She gave a brisk nod, as if he didn't make her stomach flutter. "Better."

Much better.

*Much, much better.*

At the door, she reached for her jacket where it hung on a peg on the wall. Sexy plucked up the parka first and held it open for her. Faith stood there staring at the lining of her jacket for a long stupefied second. It had been so long since a man had done anything sweet for her, she almost didn't know what to do.

Sexy shook it to get her attention. "I know it's a short walk, but you're gonna want it."

Faith turned and slipped her arms into her jacket. "Thank you."

She slung her purse over her shoulder and replaced her barriers like a force field for the one-block stroll.

Outside, the air hit Faith like a snowball, but that didn't do much to straighten out the buzz in her head. And that was fine. Good, in fact. She needed every distraction to get her through this holiday. The man beside her was a great way to start. And for the first time, Taylor's idea of Faith stepping back into the world of men held a spark of appeal.

"I really appreciate you saving my ass," Sexy said. "Can I take you to dinner this week to say thank you?"

She gave him a what-the-heck grin and caught sight of a Range Rover parked in front of her store with a fine layer of snow on it. Sexy's, no doubt. "You can say thank you right now."

"But that wouldn't be near as fun."

She paused at the front door to the hardware store. After pulling her keys from her pocket, Faith worked the lock. "How long have you been in town?"

"I don't know, couple of hours. Why?"

"Because you sure work fast."

"I won't be here long," he said. "And I know a good thing when I see it."

Somehow she was sure he'd meant "I know what I want when I see it" but was smart enough to change up the words. Faith still heard it in his tone.

She turned back to him and met his eyes. "And do you always get what you want?"

His grin grew. "I try my damnedest."

"I'll just bet you do."

Faith tried not to hold the man's confidence against him as she pushed the door open and wandered toward the cash register. The original circa 1870 wood floors creaked beneath her feet, and she let the familiarity of the store curl around her as she picked up the box holding will-call tags.

"What name is the tree under?" she asked.

"You don't know me?"

She glanced over her shoulder with a ready smile for the surprise in his voice. "Nope, sure don't."

He lifted a brow as if he didn't believe her. "Saber?"

"Sa—" All the nuances she'd picked up on over the last

fifteen minutes clicked with the name, and Faith started laughing. "Oh God. Of course."

He was a Saber son. It didn't matter which of the three sons Sexy turned out to be, they were all the same—wealthy and handsome and full of themselves. One of them had been in her class, but she couldn't remember which. And she didn't care. The men now had a reputation for rolling into town to visit their parents a couple of times a year from their fancy city digs. They flashed their money and their shiny toys. Shot those pretty smiles around town until they got laid. Then rolled right back out again.

"Oh yeah," she said on a sigh of both disappointment and self-deprecation. "It all makes sense now."

"What makes sense?" he asked.

"Nothing that would interest you." She carried the tag toward the back door leading to her enclosed patio. "Your mama's tree is right out here."

She pushed open the door and breathed deep of that amazing fresh-cut pine-tree scent. After checking the tags on a few trees, she held up the correct one like a referee in a boxing match. "And we have a winner."

Saber laughed, and the smile that lit his face would have taken Faith's breath away if she'd been sober. Or if she hadn't discovered he was a Saber.

"What were you drinking at the bar again?" he asked.

She reached through the branches to grab the trunk, then let her body weight help her pull it upright. "Only the best holiday concoction anywhere."

He reached into the tree just above her grasp and took hold of the trunk. "I'll say."

Suddenly he was close again. Close enough to feel his body heat. Close enough to smell his spicy scent mixed with fresh pine. And the whole idea of a great big Christmas O was wearing down her common sense.

She released the tree and glanced up to meet his eyes. And he was looking right at her. Right into her eyes. As if he was fully present. Not checking her out. Not already getting busy with her in his head. But right there, in the moment, with her. And he looked expectant, as if he were waiting for...something.

Since she was way out of her element, Faith took a step back. "I'm assuming a big, strong man like you can get this itty-bitty tree to your car on your own." She sidestepped him to cross the patio and unlock the gate. "I'm not in any shape to be throwing trees right now."

Sexy hefted the twelve-foot noble fir—one of Faith's largest and most expensive trees, wrapped safely in orange netting—onto his shoulder in one smooth motion.

Faith's mouth dropped open. "Well, there's one for the books. In all the years I've been selling trees, I can't say I've ever seen anyone handle one quite like that."

He sauntered toward her and paused just inside the gate—and inside her personal space. A tingle of awareness that had quickly become familiar spread through Faith again. And before she knew how it had happened, her gaze slipped to his mouth. Her mind to how his lips would feel against hers. It had been so long since she'd kissed a man. So damn long.

Maybe there was something to testing the waters again. Taking the old libido on a spin with someone who rolled out of town as easily as he rolled in. Kissing without commitment? Dating without promises? Sex for sheer pleasure?

"It's all in the setup and balance." His voice, low and soft, dragged her from the luscious thoughts, but the heat in his eyes hinted that his mind was headed in a similar direction. "If you've got that right, even you could do this."

That made her laugh, and the alcohol turned it into a giggle. "I don't think so."

"I'll teach you how if you want." The insinuation in those words quickened Faith's heart. His low, smooth tone created a heaviness between her legs. "Imagine the reaction of all the tough guys in town when you throw a baby like this on your shoulder and carry it to their car." His gaze took on a little more heat. "Let me take you to dinner, and I'll share the trick. Maybe I'll even share a couple more."

Oh wow. Everything inside her was yelling *yes, yes, yes*.

But she'd had too much common sense ruling her world for far too long for her to simply jump.

She lowered her gaze and shook her head. "Thanks anyway."

When his feet didn't move toward his car, she glanced at his face again. He was looking at her with a little bit of dismay. "You *really* don't know who I am, do you?"

She wondered if the alcohol had affected her memory. This time of year, so many family members came to town, so many previous residents returned to visit. Normally, she had a good memory. Remembering was good for business. But...

Her brows lifted. "You're a Saber."

"I'm *Grant*."

He said it as if it should mean something. Though she had no idea what. "Nice to meet you, *Grant*. I'm Faith. I'm also beat, and I have another long day ahead of me tomorrow. Say hello to Hazel for me."

He chuckled as if he found her amusing, lifted his brows, and said, "*Grant Saber?*"

"Yeah. I got that. Grant plus Saber would equal *Grant Saber*. I haven't had *that* much to drink." And she found the fact that he expected his name to be on the lips of everyone in town both comical and annoying. "Good night, *Grant Saber*."

He huffed a sound of humorous dismay and started for the street, but before he passed through the gate, he paused beside her. "Will you let me walk you home?"

That sweet pang tugged inside her again and this back and forth was driving her mad. "I *am* home." When Grant frowned and glanced toward the store, Faith added, "I live in the apartment above the store."

"Ah..." He steadied the tree on his shoulder with one hand and pulled something from his pocket with the other. "Here's my number. I won't be in town long, so use it while you can."

That did it. Now she was ticked.

Faith curled her fingers around the chain link in the gate and ignored his card. With her gaze directly on his, she offered a firm "No, thank you. *Good night*."

"You're going to want to call me when you figure out who I am."

"You're lucky I have alcohol in my system, or I wouldn't be acting this nice." That and she was too damned tired to get pissed over his arrogance. "Please leave so I can find my pillow."

He shot her one of those I'm-so-not-taking-you-seriously grins. With his gaze holding hers, he reached down to slip the card into the back pocket of her jeans. The move brought his lips within inches of hers. His warmth and scent flooded the space around her, and she felt a fundamental shift in her body. One that made her grip the gate harder to keep herself steady. His touch shot a tingle of sensation across her backside.

"When you're ready," he murmured, his voice quiet and thick, "call me. For a drink, dinner, *dessert*. Call me for...*anything*...you need." His fingers slipped across her jaw in a whisper. "Sleep tight, angel."

Then he stepped onto the sidewalk and strode to an SUV at the curb like nothing had happened, while Faith struggled to secure a gate she'd locked at least a thousand times over the years. His *"dessert"* and *"anything"* had hit the nerves he'd intended, and desire shivered through her belly. The *"angel"* touched a different place, the same one affected when he'd held her jacket.

Taylor was definitely right about one thing—both of those places in Faith had been neglected for far too long.

When she finally locked the gate, she glanced up and found him tying the tree to that shiny Range Rover. One so new it still carried the dealer's plates. She huffed and shook her head. Filling those needs by allowing herself to be used by a rich, arrogant man was not going to help her in any way.

Except to get laid.

Maybe give her that momentary escape she craved.

Possibly distract her through this painful, lonely holiday.

While also giving her some much-needed companionship, male contact, long-denied pleasure...

Faith sighed as she retraced her steps to lock the interior doors and turn off the lights, then took the stairs to her apartment above the store, thinking about Grant Saber's hot little smile. Those full lips. That tall, muscular body.

And a thread of apprehension snuck in as she reached the door to her apartment. "What the hell would I do with all that man?"

She let all the stresses of the day drain away as she wandered into her living room, hoping the alcohol would help her get a good night's sleep for a change.

With her purse and her jacket on the love seat, Faith paused at the windows and drew the blinds against the dark night still sparkling with a light snow. When she glanced toward the street, she found Grant speaking with Dwayne Urich. Since the death of his wife, Dwayne would talk to anyone who would listen for as long as they would listen. Faith gave Grant five minutes before he cut Dwayne off. Someone that self-important wouldn't waste his time with Dwayne's lonely rambles.

But as she counted down the minutes, Faith realized Grant wasn't just listening to Dwayne, he was laughing. He was engaging. The two were having a lively conversation. She had to admit, she hadn't seen Dwayne as animated in a very long time.

After ten minutes, Grant was still leaning against his car, hands in his pockets, snow layering his hair and jacket. The sight reminded her of those last days with her father and how he'd taken such joy in the visits from his closest friends.

And her anger toward the stranger's arrogant edge softened. "Maybe you're not all bad, Grant Saber."

# 3

Grant's gut hurt from laughing at the tales Dwayne spun of Holly's current high school hockey team.

He leaned his parka-covered ass against his SUV so he could keep an eye on Faith in his peripheral vision. She was watching him from a window above the hardware store. He'd known all the buildings in town had spaces above, but most had been used for offices even when Grant had lived there.

As soon as she discovered who he was, she'd be calling. The thought spilled another burst of heat through his body. If he didn't stop thinking about quieting her sassy mouth in creative ways, he was going to have to take off his jacket.

"And then..." Dwayne said, winding down his most recent story of an away game with the team. The roads home had been closed due to snow, and they had to stay in a motel overnight. "Even after eight other guys had failed, Healy decides he can reach the ground floor, with, get this—"

"Oh God, he didn't—" Grant said with humor bubbling up from his belly.

Dwayne was already nodding. "The Saber sling."

Grant doubled over laughing. Ten years later, kids were still reenacting his legendary antics in high school. When he ran out of breath, he straightened and asked, "Did he make it?"

"Nope." Dwayne chuckled. "Kids nowadays aren't like my generation. They all spend their time on video games, not out on the farm or ranch. Most don't even have chores around the house. None of them could tie a square knot to save their lives. Healy ended up ass first in the snow."

"How long did you leave him there?"

"Twenty minutes."

Grant winced. "Ooo, harsh."

Dwayne just chuckled, and Grant noticed the light in Faith's apartment go out.

"So when do you want to get started?" Dwayne asked. "I've been holding back in case something came up and you couldn't make it. Just told the boys there would be extra practice over the break. You should have heard the moans and groans. I miss the days when kids couldn't wait to get out on the ice, and I'm hoping you can bring some of that back to us."

"The sooner the better. Like I told you when we cooked this up, I'm ready."

"Perfect. I'll corral the boys. Plan on something tomorrow afternoon. Say around two?"

"I'll be there."

With a beaming grin, Dwayne shook Grant's hand and used the other to slap his bicep. "This is gonna be real special for the kids."

"My pleasure. See you tomorrow."

Dwayne turned toward the sidewalk, and Grant pushed off the car.

"And thanks for agreeing to judge the ice sculptures this year. The posters are getting printed right now. The team will be slapping them up all over the county."

As he rounded the front of his car, Grant's attention swung back to Dwayne. "What? What about ice sculptures?"

"You haven't been gone *that* long," Dwayne said, a smile in his voice. "You remember, the biggest draw of the Winter Wonderland Festival? But once word got out that you were judging, the entries poured in. That money helps with the hockey team's travel and uniform expenses. But it's looking like we'll have enough to put together a training camp over the Christmas break next year too. Could maybe even pay someone to come and give clinics."

Grant was definitely missing something. "This is the first I've heard of judging..."

Dwayne's expression clicked from happy to deer in the headlights. "Your mama told me she got the okay from you about being a judge last week."

Which would have been about the time Grant had finally given in to his mother's nagging to come home for Christmas.

Anger started to simmer beneath his skin. "My mama."

"This is one of her biggest fundraisers for the Art League. A portion of the proceeds from the ice carving goes to her charity."

"Yeah, that I remember." That fucking charity. It wasn't the charity that Grant disliked as much as it was his mother's obsession with running it. He took a deep breath and let it out in a billow of condensation. "Don't you love life's little ironies, Dwayne?"

Dwayne hesitated. "Hey, Grant, if it's a problem—"

"No, Dwayne. It's not a problem. My mama's the problem. I'll do whatever you need me to do to support you and the kids. You know that."

"It means a lot to me, kid." Dwayne smiled, but the enthusiasm was gone, and Grant knew the older man was pulling up memories from the past over the sore subject of his family and their refusal to support Grant's love of hockey.

Dwayne's gaze traveled to Grant's SUV. "Quite a ride you got there. That a Range Rover? What did that set you back, a hundred grand?"

A hundred and a half, but Dwayne didn't care. This was just an attempt to shift gears and get away from the troubling topic of family. "Something like that."

"Quite a tree you picked out. A ten footer?"

"Twelve." Grant glanced at the monster atop his vehicle, wishing he'd told his mother no to the holidays and chosen another charitable way to spend his time to get the Rough Riders' owner off his back. But Grant had thought he'd be killing two birds with one stone by doing both here. He was also four hundred miles away from those tempting Rider Girls, who were always sweeping him into the kind of distraction the team owner was tired of hearing about through the media or friends. It was probably the only drawback to signing with the team—the owner's conservative view of how players should run their life off the ice. Grant didn't mind doing what he was told when it involved his game or even his career. He did take issue with being told where to develop his morals.

But the guy was paying Grant a fucking mint, so... Here he was.

"Glad you bought it from Faith. She's had a real hard year." Dwayne's gaze turned on the hardware store, his brow pulled in concern.

"Oh yeah?" Grant looked up to see if Faith was still watching, but he couldn't tell with the light out. A hard year would explain why she was living in a tiny apartment above the store. "How's that?"

"Since her daddy passed, she's been handling everything herself."

Grant's attention snapped back to Dwayne, and shock chilled his gut. "Her daddy? When?"

"'Bout six months ago. It was a blessing in a lot of ways. He'd been battling the cancer for so long. Made a real good run of it. There was a year or two he and Faith thought he was going to beat it, but then it came back meaner than ever."

The shock transitioned into dread, and Grant's stomach dropped. "Ah, damn."

"It wasn't a surprise. He was ready to go. Faith, well, she never would have been ready. But it was long past time she got on with her own life. It ate at her daddy how much she gave up for him."

"What do you mean?"

"He got the news her first year in college. She came home that summer and never went back. That boy she went with all through high school... Well, let's just say he didn't let no grass grow under his feet. He brought the new girlfriend home with him from college the following Christmas break."

Grant took another hit to the gut. "Ouch."

Dwayne made a sympathetic sound in his throat. "She was at her daddy's side every day since she came home. They had more than a few arguments over her putting her life on hold to nurse him, but she always won." Dwayne chuckled. "A fighter, that one. Once she sets her mind to something, ain't no one gonna change it. Reminds me a lot of you that way." He patted Grant's arm. "I'm gonna let you go before we both turn into icicles."

"Sure, sure." Grant started around the front of his SUV far more subdued than when he'd first spotted Dwayne. "Hey, Dwayne? You need a ride home?"

"No, thanks, kid. These nightly walks are my quiet time with MaryAnn."

Grant nodded. "Breakfast tomorrow, then? Seven a.m.? Shelly's? I'm buyin'."

Dwayne grinned. "I'll be there."

Grant slid into the driver's seat, his mind swamped with the new information. A lot of people thought Dwayne rambled. But if they took the time to listen, they'd figure out the man said a hell of a lot in a short amount of time.

Grant turned the engine over, backed out, and started home. Facing his parents pushed his turbulent feelings about Faith and her father to the background, because Grant didn't know how to feel or what to think about everything he'd just learned. Right now, all he could focus on was what he could understand—his mother and her manipulation.

He shouldn't be surprised. Shouldn't give a damn. But by the time he pulled into his parents' driveway again, he was damn good and ready to bail on the festival and leave a check in Dwayne's mailbox instead.

He pulled the tree onto his shoulder, pushed through the front door, and turned into the living room. Then immediately dropped the tree, spreading ice and pine needles across his mother's perfectly manicured carpet.

Dual gasps touched his ears before he looked up.

"Grant Saber," his mother scolded. "What on earth is wrong with you?"

*"You"* was what he wanted to say, but he saw someone else in the room. A young woman sitting on the next cushion. Even after being away for years, Grant immediately knew who she was and why she was here.

Which only angered him more.

"What's going on?" Grant's father came in from the next room. "What in the hell happened here?" Martin Saber spread his hands, indicating the mess of the tree, but didn't wait for an answer before his glare turned on Grant. "Clean up that mess right now."

"I'll clean up my mess if you clean up yours."

"Grant." His mother's cutting, shape-up-right-this-second tone hauled Grant back to his childhood. "You remember Natalie."

Natalie Duboix, the oldest daughter of Dad's business partner. Grant remembered her because the two families had been trying to set them up for years, all with the hope of pulling Grant away from hockey and back into the family fold.

"She's organizing Winter Wonderland this year," Hazel said when he didn't answer, "and we were just talking about the possibility of you presenting the keynote speech at the banquet that always wraps up the festival."

"The answer to that would be *no*. Just like the answer to me judging the ice-sculpting contest would have been no *had I been asked*. In fact, if I'd known I was going to be manipulated while I was here, I wouldn't have come at all."

Natalie cast a dry smile at Hazel and patted her hand. "I'll just give you all some family time."

She stood and walked toward Grant. Or rather sashayed. Her tight fitted skirt made it impossible for her to do anything else. Her heels were spiked, her blouse see-through with something lace beneath. She'd always been pretty, but Natalie had become truly beautiful with age. In a word-association game, her image would elicit a response of Stepford wife—perfectly proportioned features, creamy skin, every deep brown strand of her hair curled just so.

For a second—just a split second—he wondered what she'd look like throwing Christmas trees. And his admiration for Faith's perseverance and tenacity sparked again.

Just when Grant thought Natalie would walk past without comment, she stopped beside him. Slipping her arm around his, she hugged his bicep against her breasts and surrounded him in a bubble of powdery perfume. Grant looked down into her crystal-blue eyes and realized that if he didn't know her, if they'd met somewhere else, like at a party in DC, he'd be all over the idea of getting her back to his place. She was gorgeous and refined. She reeked of money and connections and easy sex. And reminded Grant of the kind of women he'd dated when he'd taken breaks from playing with the anything-goes

Rider Girls.

"You look better than ever." Her voice was soft and alluring. "I see you on the news doing all sorts of great things for charity. Your generosity is one of the things I adore most about you. And you'll be doing a lot of good right here in your hometown if you participate." Her grin grew, and her perfectly straight, perfectly white teeth gleamed. "You can bet I'll be here to keep you company."

She squeezed his arm and continued through the living room toward the foyer, escorted by Grant's father.

As soon as the door closed behind Natalie, Hazel turned an icy glare on Grant. "What in God's name has gotten into you?"

"Eight years," he said, forcing his voice down so Natalie wouldn't hear through the many windows that looked out over the property. "You've been nagging me to come home for the holidays for *eight years*. And when I finally do, I find out the only reason you wanted me here was so you could use my name to rake in money for your charity. *That's what's gotten into me.*"

"Watch it," Martin warned, returning to the living room. "We gave you that name."

"You might have named me, but I *earned* the reputation behind the name—*despite* you."

Martin's face reddened, and he opened his mouth.

"Just calm down, everyone," Hazel said. "Let's take a second to put everything into perspective."

"I've got it all in perfect perspective, and it's damned ironic," Grant told her. "After suffering through decades of disappointment over my love of hockey, you now need me—and the fame I've earned through the sport you hate—to pull in money for your charity. All so you can look like hot shit to people in this town."

"You will *not* talk to your mother like that—"

He swung toward his father. "I'm talking to you too, Dad. You're no better."

"Get out." Martin stabbed his index finger at the door. "Right now."

"No, he's right," his mother countered before Grant could even take a step. "I'm sorry, Grant. You're right. In my defense, I have always wanted you home to have the family together, but when I heard you weren't skating over the holiday and could make it, I did leverage your visit for the good of the community. And while your success hasn't come in the way your father and I had hoped, there is no denying you have reached incredible heights in your career."

She paused, looking more contrite than Grant had ever seen her, and drew a breath. "Regardless of whether I care for hockey or not, as your mother, I'm proud. So, yes, I want you out there front and center, where everyone can see what a success you've made of your life."

No. She wanted him out there front and center so she could brag about him. So she could take some sort of credit for his success, when the truth was Grant had fought his parents every step of the way to get to this point in his career.

But he knew that look in her eyes. She wholeheartedly believed what she was saying. And there was no point in trying to get her to see that she was still lying to herself. As for Martin, Grant already knew the man would go to his grave disappointed that his middle son had gone rogue and deserted the family business.

Bottom line: Grant would always be considered a loss to his parents, no matter what he achieved.

"Please stay, son," his mother said. "You'll be doing great things for the high school team. A lot of boys here look up to you."

Like she knew anything about the high school team.

Neither she or his father had ever been to one of his games. Not one in Grant's entire life.

"Don't try to guilt me. We all know neither of you care who looks up to me or what I could do for the team. All you care about is what you care about. It's always been that way. It will, obviously, always be that way. But you're right about one thing. There are people here who respect what it took for me to get where I am. And I do want to help those people. So if I stay, I'll be staying for them."

"Grant..." His mother exhaled and shook her head. "Let this argument blow over and see how you feel about things. Your brothers will be here soon, and they're looking forward to seeing you."

Perfect. His brothers. The older one was so green with envy over Grant's career success, he constantly took cuts at Grant's game like the fucker knew what he was talking about. The younger one was so wild, Grant was shocked he was still alive. Surely the only reason he wasn't incarcerated was because their father repeatedly bailed him out.

Now Grant wished he'd thought this decision through better. But there had been a sliver of hope that his family had changed over the years. And the fact that they hadn't, that they might even be worse than they'd once been, both hurt and deflated Grant.

"This was a fuckin' bad idea," he muttered, rubbing the tension from his face. Now he felt stuck. He'd promised Dwayne. Dwayne would have promised the kids by now. And one thing Grant hated to do was let kids down. He knew how that felt and avoided it at all costs.

"Stay in the guesthouse if you need your own space," his mother added.

What fuckin' choice did he have? He could get a hotel, but the closest one was a several miles out of town and he'd end up driving back and forth all day, every day.

"I'll think about it." He bent, picked up the tree, and dragged it toward the front window, where their Christmas tree had reached toward the open-beamed ceilings for as long as he could remember. "And for the last time, stop trying to force Natalie on me. I have a life in DC. A damned good one. I'm not staying here, and no one is going to change my mind about what I do for a living. Sure as hell not a woman."

He gripped the netting and took out his frustration on the nylon, ripping it open. "Now where do you want this damn thing?"

# 4

Faith knelt on the floor at the back of the store, surrounded by miles of tangled Christmas lights. Overwhelmed, she looked up at Dwayne. "And why, exactly, did you wait until so close to Christmas to bring this to me?"

"Ah..." He grimaced and scratched his head. "I wasn't sure whether or not I was going to do it this year. And I thought I'd be able to figure it out on my own. But I'm just realizing why MaryAnn spent weeks on setting this up every year." He sighed and shook his head. "I wouldn't ask you... I know how busy you get during the holidays...but..." He lifted his gaze to Faith's and the pain there resonated with her intimately. "I can't take the darkness or the silence anymore. The holidays were so lively, so full of fun, when MaryAnn was here..."

His voice broke. He dropped his gaze to the mess on the floor with a sad laugh, but not before Faith saw his eyes glisten with tears.

Her heart broke for him. For herself. For all the Christmases ahead that she and Dwayne would have to spend without the people they loved in their lives.

Holding back her own pain, Faith pushed to her feet,

stepped over the light strands and gripped Dwayne's biceps. She worked up a smile and squeezed his arms. "I understand. Perfectly. I'll get this working for you, Dwayne. I promise."

He lifted a wobbly smile just as a young male voice bellowed Faith's name. "Auntie Faith! Auntie Faith! Where are you?"

Dwayne smiled, the expression sad. Hollow. "Caleb."

"Yeah." She dropped her arms and planted her hands on her hips. "His mom's got some work to do. He's helping me here today."

Dwayne's laugh was tired. "Oh, well...good luck with that. If you figure out a way to get him to pay more attention on the ice, let me know. Thanks for...um..."—he gestured to the equipment—"this."

"Of course."

Caleb ran past the aisle. Then his tennis shoes squeaked to a halt on the linoleum floor, and he reappeared near the end cap. "Auntie Faith, guess who's here?"

Faith grinned at the boy's ever-present enthusiasm. "Hi, Caleb. I'm fine, thanks for asking."

"But...but...but *guess* who's in *town*."

Dwayne laughed. "You gotta knock that off, kid. He's not going to put up with any fangirling."

"There you are." Taylor appeared at the end of the aisle behind her son. "Jeez, Caleb. What happened to waiting for me?"

Caleb glanced over his shoulder. "You always talk with Cody's mom *forever*."

Faith crossed her arms and looked at Taylor. "What's going on?" Man, she hoped Caleb's father hadn't started coming around. The asshole would just bail like he always did and break Caleb's heart again. "Sounds pretty exciting."

Caleb's head snapped back toward Faith. "*Grant Saber* is here," he said with the same awe and enthusiasm as Faith would have expected from him at a monster truck show. "And he's *helping* with the *team*."

The only team Caleb could have been talking about was the hockey team. No matter how hard Taylor tried, she couldn't get her nerdy boy interested in any other sport or team.

"You like that, huh?" Dwayne asked, patting Caleb's shoulder as he wandered past and down the aisle.

"Yeah," Caleb said with a tone of "duh."

"Caleb" was all Taylor had to say before the boy realized his misstep.

"I mean, yes, sir. It's awesome. He's really cool."

"Extra cool since he only came to help out the high school team but stayed over to help your club team, huh?" Dwayne asked, the first real grin lighting his eyes.

"Totally." Then suddenly, Caleb's excitement turned to concern. "He'll come again, right? I mean, he wasn't there for just today..." Caleb's worried gaze darted to Taylor. "Mom? I didn't get his autograph. I thought he'd be back."

Taylor was beaming. Caleb's disinterest in sports or even playing on the playground in favor of quieter endeavors had caused the already-introverted boy to be shoved aside for more active, more popular friends in school.

"Autograph, huh?" Faith said, shooting a questioning gaze toward Taylor. "Well, if you stick around long enough, he'll be here. He's been in at least three times a day for the last two days."

"Really?" Caleb said.

Dwayne strolled past Caleb, patting his shoulder. "Don't worry, Caleb, he's here for a few weeks. But you'd better get all that excitement out before you hit the ice this afternoon. He wants you kids focused and ready to work."

"Yes, sir," he said, serious and stoic. "I will, sir. I promise."

Dwayne chuckled, said hello to Taylor and waved good-bye to Faith.

Before Faith could ask Taylor or Caleb about Grant—more specifically why Caleb wanted his autograph—Caleb looked at Faith and said, "How old would I have to be to work here, Aunt Faith?"

Faith's brows shot up. "Well, that's new. You didn't want to have anything to do with helping out a few months ago."

"So you'll let me?"

Faith lifted her gaze to Taylor, grinning. "I'll talk to your mom about it."

"Thanks, Aunt Faith." He turned to his mother. "Can I go look at the fishing poles?"

"From hockey to fishing in a split second." A little of the excitement leaked from Taylor's expression. "Sure."

Caleb hurried in the direction of the outdoors department where Faith carried a limited supply of recreational gear for tourists, and Taylor came toward Faith.

"That's who you met at the bar the other night," she said, voice lowered. "The guy you said asked you out, right? Grant Saber?"

"Yeah." Her stomach tightened. "Why? Who is he?"

"He's a center for the Rough Riders." Her voice and expression held as much excitement as her son's.

But Faith was having a hard time placing the Rough Riders. "I'm guessing that's a hockey team?"

That accounted for his great build. This celebrity Faith couldn't appreciate was obviously why he'd thought she should have known him. It also seemed to be what he was looking for every time he came into the store.

"It's an NHL team, Faith."

"Don't say that like I'm supposed to know. You know I don't have time to watch television. And I only pretended to watch sports to keep Dad company."

"Why has he been coming in? Did he ask you out again? Because you should go. He's hot. And he's loaded."

"And he's just looking to get laid like his brothers." She gave Taylor a look. "You hate his brothers. You turn them down every time they're in town. Why would you suggest I go out with Grant?" Suddenly, she was mad. "Do you really think I'm so bad off that I need to go out and fuck some slutty player? Because I've got more important things—"

"No." Taylor's hand closed over Faith's forearm, her voice level again, her eyes serious. "That's not what I meant."

Faith shut her mouth and lifted both hands to her face to rub at her eyes. "I'm sorry. I'm tired." She'd lost sleep over Grant. Grant and all the little fantasies he'd stirred in her head. She swept a gesture over the lighting extravaganza equipment. "And Dwayne just dumped this project on me."

She crouched and started winding light strands from palm to elbow, palm to elbow.

"What I meant," Taylor said, "is that he's not his brothers. He's never been in town. This is the first time he's been back since he went pro."

Now she was sort of impressed that he hadn't told her that he was a pro hockey player, or that he was here to help coach the local teams when he'd come into the store. And she didn't want to be impressed. Because she didn't have time or patience for this shit. "That doesn't matter. He's still looking to get laid. What is it about these guys? Do they think we're all hard up because we're out here in the boonies? It may be true, but it's still insulting."

Taylor laughed. Hard. Which brought a reluctant smile to Faith's lips.

"It is really cool to see Caleb excited about something, though," Faith said. "I haven't seen his eyes light up like that in a long time."

"Right?" Taylor said. "So is that why Grant's been in here so much?"

Faith shrugged as she finished rolling a strand, secured the end and started on another. She'd be here the rest of the day untangling these things. "Hey, Caleb," she yelled through the store. "If you come untangle these lights for me, I'll pay you."

"Stop avoiding the question," Taylor said.

When Caleb didn't yell back or appear, Faith muttered, "So much for working here. Guess I'll be hiring Billy Danielson after all." Then she told Taylor, "Grant's staying with his parents. Apparently, they don't get along all that well, so he picked up some odd jobs around the house to stay busy and away from them. He's always here picking up supplies and asking for advice."

"And? Are you helping him?"

"Sure." She smiled up at Taylor now. "I tell him to search YouTube."

"Faith..." Taylor dropped her arms and rolled her eyes.

"I don't have time to babysit him. He's a grown-ass man. He can figure it out himself."

Taylor heaved an exasperated sigh.

"And speaking of YouTube, when can we get together to figure something out for me? I'm serious, Taylor. I'm bleeding money faster than it's getting pumped back in. It's only a matter of time. Do you want me to sell this place and move away from you and Caleb? Because that's about where my life is headed at the moment."

A pained look came over Taylor's face. Faith hated to paint such a bleak picture, but she was very serious. And that was what Faith saw in her future.

"Fine." Taylor crossed her arms again. "You need to think of a project, and I need to get some things done so I can focus on teaching you the steps—"

Faith didn't hear anything Taylor said after that, because Grant sauntered around the corner and into their aisle. His gaze fastened on Faith with bold deliberateness and made her stomach jump to her throat.

"Do I hear you ladies talking about YouTube?" he asked, wandering toward them. Taylor spun around, but Grant's gaze stayed locked on Faith in a way that made her mouth go dry. A slow smile tipped his mouth. "Because I'd be real interested in getting in on a video with y'all."

A laugh bubbled up from nowhere. "Y'all?" Faith said, hiding her nerves behind sarcasm. "You picked up a Southern accent in the last..." She pretended to look at a nonexistent watch. "What? Three, four hours?"

He laughed. "You're so funny."

"I try." She pulled her gaze off all the muscle stretching the soft fabric of his Henley and grabbed another string of lights. "I need something to keep me from"—*fantasizing about you*—"going insane."

"Hi," Taylor said, extending her hand. "I'm Taylor, Caleb's mom."

"Grant," was all he offered as they shook. "Yeah, saw him messing around with the fishing poles. He told me you were back here." He took his hand back and slipped his thumb into the front pocket of his jeans, which drew Faith's gaze to an area she had no business looking at. "Great kid. Little hyper for hockey, but if I can get him to channel it, he's going to streak across the ice."

Taylor laughed. "If you get him to channel it, I'll pay handsomely for the secret." She looked at Faith. "I'd better go find him before he breaks something." Then she told Grant, "Nice to meet you."

"You too."

When his gaze settled on Faith again, he grinned. And it was that expectant grin. The one that said he was waiting for her to go all batshit crazy over him.

"What have you got there?" she asked instead, glancing at the rusted faucet he held in his hand. "And how are you finding so many things that need fixing at your parents' house? That place looks like a pristine mansion from the outside."

"Kitchen faucet," he said, "and it's not from the main house, it's from the guesthouse. That's where I'm staying. And when I'm fixing something, neither of my parents bitch at me. So I'm happy to do it."

"That has to suck."

He lifted a shoulder but broke eye contact and studied the faucet. "Whatever." He refocused on her. "Are you going to wind all those yourself?"

"I tried to tempt Caleb with a paycheck, but those fishing reels must have really caught his eye."

"I'll help." He moved forward. "And you don't even have to pay me."

She smirked. "Oh no?"

He dropped into a crouch, looked her directly in the eye, and grinned. "I'm more into trades."

Setting aside the faucet, he dropped to his butt, crossed his legs, and grabbed the tail end of a light strand.

"We're not trading anything," she clarified.

"That remains to be seen."

"You must have better things to do."

"Than sit here and look at you?" he asked. "Nope. Notta one." When Faith just shook her head, he asked, "So what's your project? The one you were talking to Taylor about?"

Faith's stomach tightened. "How long were you eavesdropping?"

"Why? Saying things you don't want me to hear? About me maybe?"

"*Pffft*. We weren't talking about you."

"If you say so. But it would probably be better for you to just tell me about the video you're planning, because I'm sure your version would be tamer than the things I have rolling around my brain right now."

"And why are you so sure of that?" She was caught between annoyance at his arrogance and amusement at the lengths he was going to gain her attention. "Because I live in the boondocks, you don't think I can think just as dirty as you?"

His hands halted in the middle of winding a strand. He lifted his brows in a teasing expression, but his pretty eyes took on a little shadow of heat. "Should we compare notes?"

Man, that voice. The smooth, low rumble settled heat low in her gut. But she chirped, "No, thanks."

And he chuckled, refocusing on the lights. "Hey, I'm really sorry to hear about your dad."

The warm, authentic tone of his voice drew her head up.

He glanced at her, then back at the lights. "I didn't know him well, but he was always real nice to me."

The sadness that always came with the reminder of her father's death weighed heavy in her heart. "Thanks. He was an amazing man."

They continued to wind lights in silence for a minute or two, but the time stretched into an eternity while Faith kept trying to figure him out.

When she couldn't and her frustration won out, Faith tied off another strand and tossed it into the growing pile. "Why are you sitting on the floor winding lights?"

He looked up. "I'm helping."

She tipped her head and gave him a come-on look.

He grinned, shrugged. "Maybe I'm trying to come up with a way to ask you out that you can't refuse." He darted a glance at her from beneath those thick lashes. "Maybe I'm hoping if you get to know me a little, you'll say yes. Maybe—"

"Maybe you don't want to go home," she finished for him.

"Maybe. But those other things are true too." He tossed another rolled strand into the pile. "I'm dying to know what project you've got planned with this mess."

She sighed—partly because of the mess in front of her and

partly because over the last couple of days, she'd grown to like the guy. And she didn't want to like him. "This isn't my proj—"

Something clicked in her head. Her hands froze. And she looked at the pile again, but this time she saw something other than a headache. She saw an opportunity.

"What just put that spark in your eye?" Grant asked.

She met his gaze, and when she found true interest there, she explained her thoughts about following Taylor's example on YouTube. "Taylor makes really good money doing it. Granted, she talks about a totally different topic, and my knowledge may not generate the same interest, but..."

"But you've got to try." He leaned back against a shelf, stretched out his legs, and crossed his feet at the ankles. Then met her eyes as he tossed more lights into the pile. "Because from what I heard, it sounds like you don't have much of a choice."

Her shoulders fell, and she looked away, ashamed to be stuck in this spot. Worse, she hated telling a stranger how desperate she was. Especially a stranger who had more money than he knew what to do with. "I'll figure it out."

"I'm sure you will," he said, his voice confident and sincere. "But you might figure it out faster if you let me help." When she shot him an exasperated look, he held up both hands. "No ulterior motive. Okay, other than staying as far away from my parents as possible. And, yeah, maybe I'd like to get to know you better. I never got the chance in high school. That Brady kid had you hog-tied."

"So you're the Saber who was in my class."

"Guilty. And I know a little about video. Shooting, cutting, and editing it. Getting it up online. That's what you want help with, isn't it?"

"Partly, yes." Faith wondered when he was going to throw in his professional hockey player status. When he was going to mention how much money he had. When he'd start dropping the names of other famous people he hung with in the big city.

He grabbed another strand of lights and started winding. "And..."

"I knew it," she said. "Here it comes."

"I'd also like to do something to cheer up Dwayne."

Faith frowned. "How'd you know this all came from Dwayne?"

"I saw him leaving. And who else in town has enough equipment for a freaking Christmas in Fantasia?"

"Good point."

"It's a hard time of year for him since MaryAnn passed. I know it would mean a lot to him if he could get this working for her. For the people in town who have looked forward to it every year for decades."

Ah, crap... Faith sighed heavily. He had to be handsome *and* hot *and* sweet?

"What?"

She just shook her head.

"Too proud?"

"What?" she asked.

"Are you too proud to accept help?" he asked.

She pressed her lips together.

He laughed, nodded. "I sorta figured that one out the night we met."

"Shut up."

After tying off the last strand of lights, he tossed them into a pile. He got to his feet, waited for Faith to finish her strand, then offered a hand to help her up.

She took it and immediately regretted it. He was big and strong and warm. And the intimacy of the simple touch crushed another barrier between them. Then he pulled her to her feet with enough force to tip her off-balance, and she fell into him with a squeak. Her chest hit his; their thighs bumped.

She pulled in a shocked breath and tried to ease away, but he'd already slipped his arm around her waist and held her tight. Their bellies pressed. Their hips aligned.

"Grant..."

*Grant what?* Her mind told her to tell him to let her go. But her body didn't want to have anything to do with that idea.

"Still have my number?" he asked.

But the words didn't register in Faith's head. All she could focus on was every point where their bodies connected. The way his forearm felt low on her back. The heat of his hand curved around her waist. The way a few of his fingers touched flesh where her shirt had ridden up. The thickness of his thigh between hers.

"Faith?"

She glanced up. Oh, shit—*wrong*. Wrong, wrong, wrong. He was looking down at her, his lips right there. *Right. There.*

Faith had forgotten how to breathe.

She watched his lips as he spoke again. "Do you still have my number?"

"No." She forced herself to at least *sound* like she was in control. "I threw it out."

His lips kicked up in a lopsided grin and his straight, white teeth contrasted with his tanned skin. He released her hand and reached around to his back pocket but still held her tight against his body. Then his hand came back, stroking her hip, rounding behind her, and sliding over her ass.

Tingles seared her skin. Heat flooded every inch of her body below the waist. She sucked a breath. "Grant—"

"There," he said, pulling his hand from her pocket and loosening the arm around her waist. "Now you have it again."

He released her but let his hand rest on her hip an extra second before leaning away. Just when Faith thought she had her feet back under her, he lifted a hand and brushed a lock of hair off her forehead, then tucked it behind her ear.

Faith closed her eyes. She couldn't help it.

His knuckles grazed her cheekbone before he murmured, "Call me, beautiful. We'll get your video made. Get you back on your feet."

She swallowed and shored up her strength before she opened her eyes again.

Just in time to see him turn the corner out of the aisle and disappear.

# 5

Grant pulled into a parking spot at the end of the street and watched customers come and go from St. Nicholas Hardware. It had been four days since he'd almost kissed Faith, right there in the middle of her damned store. Not only hadn't she called him to help with her pet project, but she continued to treat him as if the scorching heat between them was a figment of his imagination.

In truth, he was starting to believe it. He was starting to believe that he'd lost his ability to read a woman. That he was seeing and feeling things that weren't there only because he wanted them so badly.

This was a simple matter of wanting what he couldn't have. That was all. He'd never had to chase a woman, and his competitive streak just wouldn't give up until she admitted she wanted him. At this point, he didn't even care if he slept with her or not. He could get sex anywhere. He just wanted her to give. To acknowledge who and what he was. To show a sliver of real interest.

Then he was sure this ridiculous infatuation would end.

He climbed from the SUV, pocketed his keys, and pulled on

his Braves ball cap before strolling toward the store. Grant checked out the front windows of other shops and returned friendly hellos from pedestrians. This was something he did miss about small-town life. And, he had to admit, he also found a soothing sort of rhythm in being able to focus on a project or a practice. On the quiet country setting. On the sounds of nature. All without a million other pressures on his mind.

He hadn't realized he'd missed it until now.

As Christmas approached, now less than a week away, Faith's store seemed busier every time he stopped in. That was great for Faith. Not so great for Grant. When she was busy, she barely gave him the time of day. On the occasions when things were slow, he'd been able to cajole her into helping him get what he needed for whatever project he'd adopted. Though, he hadn't been able to hold her interest any longer.

He was beginning to think he'd blown it by pushing her that day—even though he hadn't pushed her near as far as he'd wanted to. He cursed his lack of finesse. But he was who he was. He didn't like or want slow and sweet. Which made him question his own judgment every time he had a dirty thought about "the sweetest girl in town."

*"Because I live in the boondocks, you don't think I can think just as dirty as you?"*

Her words jumped to mind, followed by a wicked flash of heat from head to toe.

"A man could dream," he muttered under his breath.

Regardless of whether she turned out to be the biggest prude he'd ever met or the nastiest lay he'd ever coveted, Faith Nicholas was very different from any woman he'd ever been interested in. But he was pretty sure the only reason he kept coming back was her impish little tendency to pretend he didn't exist until he put himself directly in her way and forced her to acknowledge him.

Passing the Holly Jolly Chocolatier, Grant glanced at the

artistic displays of chocolates in the windows. He was three steps past when his feet halted and spun him around almost before he understood why. But something he'd heard in the hardware store earlier this week triggered in his mind, and Grant backtracked, turning into the store.

He only had the door open three inches when the warm, chocolate-scented air reached out and grabbed hold, dragging him the rest of the way in. He was having a *Willie Wonka & the Chocolate Factory* flashback when he closed the door behind him.

"Well, look who's here." Jemma came out of the back with her dark hair tied up in a ponytail, her bright blue eyes sparkling, and her white apron smeared with chocolate. "Heard you were back in town. How's the big shot?"

He grinned. "Hey, Jemma. Man, you still look sixteen."

"Oh, go on."

"No, really. You're throwing me back to high school, only in a much better way than the first time around."

She laughed. "You've come a long way since high school. Got a lot to be proud of. Dwayne says you're pitching in to help out the hockey team."

"Word still travels fast around here."

"Like lightning."

Grant chuckled, hoping word of his identity had finally reached Faith. "Happy to do it."

"What can I get you? I have a fresh batch of that marzipan your mama loves. Makes a great stocking stuffer."

"Sure, I'll take some. Can never hurt to please my mom, right? But I'm here because I understand Faith has an addiction to your chocolate."

"Faith." Jemma lifted her brows and tried way too hard to look innocent. "Oh? Did she say what, exactly, she was addicted to?"

"No. I overheard her talking about it to a friend at the store.

She's given me a lot of help this week while I've been working on my parents' house, and I was thinking I'd bring her a little thank-you. Something she likes."

Jemma pursed her lips, scrunching them sideways, her gaze cast down.

He knew that look: the naughty, guilty one.

"I'm also trying to soften her up so she'll let me take her out," Grant added hopefully. "Some days, I swear I'm invisible."

Jemma's smooth brow pulled into a deep vee. "That's not like Faith. You may not think she's paying attention, but she knows everything that's happening around her. Everything that's happening in the store. When you think 'mind like a steel trap,' you think Faith."

He was having a hard time seeing that. "Can you help me out?"

Ten minutes later, he jogged up the brick steps to St. Nicholas Hardware and pushed through the door to a chorus of loud male voices.

"Stop, both of you," Faith cut in, her voice distinctly female and clearly authoritarian. But Grant had come to recognize the dry sarcasm edging her tone. "St. Nicholas Hardware is an inclusive safety zone for all fans, Wolfpack and Tar Heels alike."

"What the hell does a ram have to do with being a Tar Heel anyway? And what kind of name is Rameses?" Leon Simms chided Mike Lowry. "Those boys paint his horns blue? Doesn't anyone call the ASPCA? Or PETA?"

"It's pronounced ram-sees, Mike, and you know it," Faith said while she rang up and bagged his items. "Don't be starting trouble for the sake of trouble, now."

"That's right," Leon said. "Listen to the lady. She knows what she's talkin' 'bout."

"I do know what I'm talking about," Faith said. "Which is

how I also know you ask Mike the same questions every year when the Tobacco game comes up, just to rile him."

Mike pointed at Leon. "You do. Every year."

"That's because it works. Every year."

A chorus of laughter filled the store, and Grant was grinning at the exchange and Faith's smooth control over everyone and everything that happened in here as he wandered into her peripheral vision. Joe Sheridan came toward the register with a customer close behind and rang up some paint.

Faith's attention was on the credit processor waiting for the receipt, when her gaze slid left and caught sight of Grant. And she smiled. The lift to her lips, the crinkle at the corners of her eyes, they made her look cute and sweet and mischievous all at the same time. Grant was hoping to pull out more of the mischievous side. She knew he was coming in every day to see her, and she liked it. Knowing that gave him the strangest buzz. One equal to the thrill he got every time he took in the smoking way the woman wore her jeans and the way she filled out a tee shirt. But the way she kept her interest in him on lockdown frustrated the hell out of him.

"Well, look at that." She tore the receipt off the machine and placed it in front of Mike for his signature, never taking her eyes off Grant. "Real trouble just blew in."

He chuckled, crossed his arms, and waited. Faith's gaze drifted to the bag he held in his hand, then jumped back to his face with a hint of surprise, an edge of question.

"Grant," Leon said. "You're a State fan, ain't that right?"

"Don't put words in his mouth," Mike told Leon. "I happen to know Grant's a UNC fan just like my boy Bobby, ain't you, Grant?"

"My good sense tells me to stay out of this conversation," Grant said.

"Smart," Joe said without turning from the register.

A young kid Grant didn't know came up to the front

carrying five different wrenches and laid them on the counter near Faith. He wore a polo shirt with the hardware store's logo, and he was out of breath, sweating, his face red with worry. "What about these? Is it any of these?"

Leon and Mike stopped their argument to peer at the group of tools. Joe finished his sale and joined them, looking over Faith's shoulder. All of them studied the wrenches like they were some archeological relics.

"No, no, Billy." Leon frowned over at the kid, who couldn't have been more than sixteen. "Didn't you listen to me? The left-handed box-end wrench is on aisle twelve, a third of the way down, between the left-handed monkey wrench and the left-handed magnet wrench. You can't miss it."

Laughter bubbled up, and Grant had to bite his lip to keep it in. The poor kid wiped at the sweat on his forehead.

"No, Leon," Joe said. "Aisle fourteen, bottom shelf on the right at the end cap, next to the—"

"Foghorn tuning pipe," Faith finished, nodding at the kid. Her expression solemn, she patted his shoulder. "It's all right, Billy. Try again."

As soon as the kid disappeared into the maze of aisles, Leon, Mike, Joe, and Faith broke into smiles.

"He's a keeper," Leon said, voice low. "How long has he been looking for that thing now? This has to be a record."

Faith gave Joe's shoulder a push. "Put the kid out of his misery, will you? If he doesn't want to belt you or quit, he can keep the job until school starts again."

Leon and Mike said good-bye to Grant on their way out, and Faith turned to him, her grin still bright from the prank they'd collectively pulled on the new kid. "Well, good afternoon, Mr. Saber. I was starting to think I might have to go a full twenty-four hours without seeing that handsome face. What could *possibly* need fixing at your parents' house today?"

*That.* That "handsome" was one of those mixed messages

she tossed out every time he was here. The ones that didn't say she was interested, but didn't say she wasn't. And they were making him crazy. They were keeping him up at night. *She* was keeping him up at night.

No woman *ever* kept him up at night.

"I hope there's something to fix so I have an excuse to come back later. But I won't know until I get there. I was at the rink working with the kids this morning."

"Oh, right. Mr. Turner was in earlier. Said Colby had a few extra hockey practices over the break."

He nodded. Waited. And got nothing. No recognition, no excitement, no indication that she knew anything about him.

Screw the small-town gossip mill. The one time Grant needed it, the damn thing broke down.

"You look good in red," she said, her gaze on his hat, a sassy little smile tipping her mouth. "Way better than orange. Just sayin'."

He'd been wearing this goddamned Atlanta Braves hat for *four days,* and this was the first time she'd mentioned it. At first he'd thought the colors were too similar, both blue caps with different brim colors. Sure, they had different emblems, but he was trying to give the girl the benefit of the doubt. She had a shitstorm pummeling her life, after all. But now he was starting to wonder if that "mind like a steel trap" comment was truer than he realized.

He put his hand over his heart. "Swear on my honor, I've seen the error of my ways and am now a die-hard Braves fan."

"Hallelujah," she said.

"So you'll go out with me now, right?"

She sighed and stepped out from behind the counter, passing Grant with a breezy "I've got inventory to stock. Good luck finding something to fix today."

He was mesmerized by that sweet sway of her hips and the way her ass looked in those washed-out jeans. She wore some type of cowboy boots, and her sweater was a deep, bright pink and cropped, showing her trim waist and flowing curves that made Grant's mouth water. After less than a week, he was intrigued by her simple but authentic and unapologetic style. It fit her attitude and her personality, and Grant found that more refreshing every day.

Which led to today. To showing up spontaneously with no purpose, holding chocolates.

What in holy hell had happened to him?

He followed her as if she were his magnet. "Free for lunch?"

"Nope, too much to do."

"What if I bring it here?"

"No, thanks. I really don't have time to stop."

"Then you might like these chocolates I picked up next door. They're bite-size, and you can eat them on the go. They're also part of Jemma's private reserve."

Her feet halted, and she stood there frozen a second before she spun on him, took a fistful of his shirt, and pulled him into an aisle.

"Whoa, girl." He chuckled the words, thrilled he'd finally gotten a reaction out of her. "If I'd known chocolate was the key to getting your attention, I'd be a regular at Jemma's by now."

She let go of his shirt and crossed her arms. "You're playing me. Jemma would never give you access to her private reserve."

"Baby, I know *you* seem to be immune to my charms, but not every woman is."

She leaned one shoulder against a shelf. "You're not going to go away, are you?"

He mirrored her, loving this tiny sliver of her complete and total attention. He'd never had to work so hard to get something so simple in his entire life. But the zing he felt all through his body when they really connected was well worth the effort. "You're not going to cave, are you?"

She grinned, a sexy, flirty little grin that shocked Grant all the way to the pit of his stomach. "Must be hard for a handsome stud like you not to have every woman drop at your feet."

He exhaled and offered a melodramatic "I can't tell you how refreshing it is to be understood."

She laughed. Her eyes twinkled. And, God, something really different was happening here. Some wild sort of chemistry he'd never had with any other woman. And he hadn't even kissed her.

"All right, hot shot, I'll indulge you in your game. What have you got in there?"

"Just your favorites."

She shook her head. "Jemma wouldn't tell you my favorites."

"The way she wouldn't tell me about her reserve collection?"

She smirked.

Man, he was having way too much fun. He opened the bag and peered in at the chocolates. The rich, intoxicating scent hit him, and he closed his eyes, inhaling deeply. "Mmmm. Damn, that's better than a drug."

"Tease," she muttered.

He opened his eyes. "I do have Tease in here. Not too sweet, not too rich, but just right to leave you wanting more."

She sighed as if she were barely tolerating him.

"I also have Long, Slow, Deep, Wet Kiss." He let his gaze fall to her mouth and licked his bottom lip. "Mmm. This chocolate couldn't compare to the real thing with you."

She took a deep breath, ready to blow him off. "Grant—"

"Let's see." He returned his gaze to the bag. "I suppose it would be appropriate to move on to Nip, Tug, Suckle. Mmm-hmm. And oh, wow, then we dive into the really good stuff."

Lifting his gaze from the bag, he met her eyes directly, deliberately, and was a little surprised to find her lids heavy, her eyes lusty. He'd begun to believe she was truly unaffected by him.

"This is a little quick for my taste," he murmured. "I'd rather build slower, savor longer, explore in depth, but I also aim to please, so let's skip to your next favorite—First Penetration." He closed his eyes as the idea slid through him in a heat wave. "Mmmm. *Damn*. Always so good."

She heaved a sigh. "All right, Saber. You've had your fun for the day. I really have to—"

"Long and Slow, one of my favorites, right along with Deep and Hard. Both have so much pleasure potential, don't you think? All leading to the Peak, the Break, and...Ecstasy."

He was pretty sure he'd done nothing but turn himself on and reached into the bag with the intention of torturing her by eating the chocolate himself. He held out one little dark square decorated with a single yellow flower petal. "But wait, what's this?"

"Bareback," she said, her gaze hot, almost challenging, on his. "The ultimate sweet ride."

A lightning strike of lust cut him straight down the middle. "Ah. Right."

He pulled another. This square a little lighter and topped with a purple pansy. "And this?"

"Fling." Her lips curved a little. "Leave your chocolate-commitment fears behind. This bold baby is here to satisfy when you're interested."

He laughed softly and held the chocolate higher, like a gem to the light. "I should have known you'd have these memorized." Lowering the square, he dropped it into the bag and shook his head. "Oooo, so much possibility. Too bad it will all be wasted."

She was grinning, the look a little smug. "Wasting Jemma's special reserve will earn you a fate worse than death." She pushed off the shelf and, with one quick swipe, grabbed the bag from his hand. "I'd hate to see something like that happen to a guy as thoughtful as you." She turned toward the back of the store. "Thanks, handsome. Have a great day."

Grant opened his mouth to argue and took a step after her.

"Faith!" They both turned toward the voice. "Faith, Faith, look." The kid they'd been messing with jogged up to her, carrying a handful of large sheets of paper. His wide eyes darted between Grant and Faith. "George just dropped these posters off, and *look*."

By the way the kid was pointing at something on the page while giving Grant those starstruck eyes, Grant was sure those were the posters announcing his participation with the festival and the hockey team.

He grinned, his ego inflated. The anticipation of Faith finding out he was a sports star filled him with a ridiculous level of excitement and satisfaction.

"What?" she asked, looking over the poster before telling the kid, "Just put them up in the window where we always put the local promotions."

"No," the kid said, then pointed to Grant. "It's him. He's...*look*."

Faith laughed, the sound light and bubbly and truly humor filled. "God, you are adorable," she told the kid. Then to Grant, she said, "Give him an autograph before you leave, will you?"

She turned and continued toward the back room. Confusion shocked Grant's brain still for a long second. He looked at the kid, said, "I'll catch you on my way out," then caught up with Faith and slipped his hand around her elbow. "You wait just a damn minute."

She had a chocolate in her hand and took a bite. Her eyes closed in a look of bliss, and the hum of pleasure that rolled from her throat seemed to funnel blood straight to his groin.

"You know who I am?"

When she opened her eyes, a hint of humor edged the heat

there. "Grant Saber, son of Hazel and Martin Saber. Center for the DC Rough Riders. Benched for a shoulder injury but headed back to the ice any day now. Bachelor extraordinaire. And an amazing judge of chocolate. I've really got a lot to do."

When she tried to turn, he pulled her to face him again. "How long? How long have you known?"

"Since the day you offered to help me with Dwayne's lights." She lifted the bag and gave him a sweet grin. "Thanks again."

He didn't let go. "Then why are you still resisting me?"

She turned to fully face him, serious now. "That spotlight has fried your humility. Out here, in the real world, not all women fall on their backs just because you're good-looking, built, and rich."

He immediately thought of Dillon and how quickly he'd replaced Faith after so many years together. Guilt snuck in. And, yeah, maybe a little shame too. Because he *was* expecting his status as a star NHL player to impress her out of her pants. It had always worked in the past.

To lighten the conversation, he added, "You forgot famous, charming, and funny."

"The famous part goes against you in my opinion. As far as charming and funny goes, those traits seem highly variable, depending on whether you're getting what you want or not."

"You don't know me well enough to say that."

"Grant, you've been in my store three or four times a day for a week. That's more than I see most of my customers in three months, and I know their life stories."

He frowned, thinking back over the week. Wondering what he'd said or done to make her think she'd figured him out. Hell, he hadn't even figured himself out.

"I'm sorry I'm not speechless over your star status. I just happen to believe that all the great stuff in here"—she tapped his chest with an index finger—"is what really matters. And you've got enough stuff in here to make your hockey stats and your bank balance and your shiny new Range Rover pale by comparison."

The woman turned him inside out on a dime. To push aside the uneasy feelings in the pit of his stomach, he said, "Whoa. Let's leave my Rover out of this."

She laughed and gave him an exasperated shake of her head. "Go on. Leave me alone so I can get some work done. We don't all get R&R for a shoulder injury."

She tried to turn away.

He should let her. He knew he should. But he held on and pulled her to face him again. When he opened his mouth to say...he didn't even know what, a customer wandered out of one aisle and into another.

Grant walked Faith backward the last few feet into the storage room and kicked the door closed.

"Grant..." she said, in that I-don't-have-time-for-this sort of way.

But he turned and pushed her up against a wall. Her laughter died, and heat sparked in her eyes. She lifted her hands, pressing them against his chest, but didn't push him away. He leaned in until their hips met and their thighs brushed. Her breath quickened. Her pupils dilated. And the look on her face... She wanted him just as badly. She just didn't know how to jump.

But Grant couldn't keep playing this game with her. He didn't do games at all, yet she'd dragged him into this one. And as enticing as it might be, Grant didn't have enough time. Or enough patience.

She needed a push.

He slid an arm behind her and drew her in with a forearm at the base of her spine. Her softness pressed against his growing erection, and pleasure washed through the lower half of his body. He moaned softly and rocked against her until she made the same sound. Until her lids grew heavy. Until her fingers curled into his shirt. Until she murmured his name in that voice that said *make me come.* "Grant..."

"Is this what you want, Faith? If you want me to take control, I will. But if I lead, I'll do it my way."

Her gaze jumped from his mouth to his eyes. "What's...your way?"

For a split second, he considered lying. He thought about telling her what she wanted to hear just to get her into bed. He wanted her that badly. And that reality—more than anything else—pushed a very harsh description from his mouth.

"If I did it my way, I'd do you right here, right now, up against this wall."

Her breathing picked up. Her eyes sparked with surprise and lust.

"I'd cover your mouth with my hand and drive into you until you snapped in a screaming climax. All while the whole store, the whole fucking town of Holly, was just six inches away. And it would be our sweet little secret. One you'd think about every time you walked into this room."

She made a sound in her throat. Her lids dipped. She licked her lips.

"You like that idea," he said, "don't you?" And wasn't that the biggest fucking surprise and the hottest rush?

Her gaze darted away. "I...I don't know. I can't think..."

"Then imagine"—he told her, pushing harder, half hoping she shoved him off and walked away, half hoping she told him to take her right then—"because I talk as dirty as I fight, and I fuck as hard as I play."

She breathed a moan, and her eyelids slid closed.

But it was the feel of her body softening, of the way she started moving with him, not against him, that finally blocked his ability to think.

"Oh, baby," he groaned, relishing that moment of surrender.

"*So...fucking...sweet*. Feel it?" he whispered. "Feel how good it is? Imagine how much better it could be. Naked. Skin on skin."

She made the slightest shake of her head. "I...wouldn't know what to do with you."

He lifted a hand to her jaw and tilted her head back until she opened her eyes to his. "Yes. You would. You're already doing it." He let his gaze slide to her mouth. "Fuck, I want to taste you."

"Grant..." she said in that voice that made him want to rip her clothes off. "I'm not... I can't..."

"Stop talking yourself out of it and just fucking kiss me already."

But Grant couldn't wait anymore. He slid his hand from her jaw, around the back of her neck, and pulled her in. Too rough. Too harsh. Too fast. The way he did everything in life.

Faith gasped, and Grant took the moment to dive in. He kissed her hard. Kept her lips open with the pressure so he could stroke his tongue into her hot mouth and taste her, the way he'd wanted to taste her since she'd met his eyes at the bar with that sassy smirk.

A mewl rose from her throat and fueled Grant's fire. He pushed his hand into her hair and closed his fingers to keep her there, keep her mouth open so he could taste her and taste her and taste her. Knowing the second he let go, she'd scamper away and never come near him again.

Part of him wanted that. More than he realized until now. Because she tasted like heat and chocolate. Her mouth was sweet and soft and plump. And suddenly, her mouth wasn't enough. He wanted more. Wanted his mouth on skin. Wanted skin on skin. Wanted his mouth on her pussy, fucking her the way he was tasting her.

And then she kissed him back. She leaned into him, her fingers curled into his shirt, her nails scraped his skin and her tongue... God, the tentative way she tasted him back made

Grant *insane*. He growled, tipped his head and demanded more.

A murmur broke into his fantasy. Someone calling Faith's name. Only it wasn't him—his mouth was way too busy to talk.

Faith moaned and turned her head, breaking the kiss. She reached out and slapped at the lock on the door, then exhaled and pressed her face against Grant's neck.

He opened the hand in her hair and cradled her head, feeling the silkiness of the strands for the first time.

"Faith?" The male voice, clear and much closer now, jolted Grant back to reality. He lifted his head and looked toward the door.

The handle turned, and Faith tried to pull away like a guilty kid. But Grant held on while the knob jerked back and forth, and the door remained closed.

"What's up, Joe?" Faith said.

"You okay?"

The what's-going-on tone in his voice made Grant dart a look at Faith. She met Grant's gaze.

And smiled. A small, secretive, embarrassed little smile that knocked Grant's heart on its ass.

"Yeah," she said, lifting her fingers to her mouth where her lips were reddened and puffy from Grant's kiss. A sight that only made him hungrier. "You know, just one of those days."

"Oh." Pause. "Okay." Pause. "Do you want me to have the Makita rep come back after the holidays?"

She stiffened and turned her attention to the door. When Grant didn't let her go, she closed her eyes. "No." She winced. "Can you have him wait? I just need a minute."

"Of course. No problem."

They stood there a long moment, their bodies pressed together, until all auditory signs of Joe were gone. Then she lifted her gaze to Grant. And now guilt filled the pretty blue irises. "I'm sorry."

He knew instantly she was talking about more than the interruption. And his heart dropped to the pit of his stomach.

"This isn't..." she started. "I'm not... I mean, I can't..." She squeezed her eyes shut and whispered, "Shit."

Shit was right. He hadn't been this turned on, this fast, in for-freaking-ever.

Reality was such a fucking bitch.

"Faith?" Joe called from somewhere in the store.

She exhaled heavily, turned her head, and bit out, "What?"

The uncharacteristic snap in her voice was Grant's signal to put an end to this. He loosened his hold and eased back.

"Sorry, honey," Joe said, "but the register is wigging out again. Only you can get it to behave."

"Okay." Faith closed her eyes, crossed her newly freed arms, and rubbed her forehead. "I'll be right out."

She looked at Grant with apology pouring from her eyes. "I'm sorry, I have to—"

"I get it," he cut her off, trying to pretend the rejection didn't matter. Because they both knew it wasn't the store keeping her from jumping into the deep end with him. "Life's demanding."

She dropped her hand and looked between the door and Grant again before she walked out, leaving the door open.

Disappointment pierced Grant's gut. A kind of disappointment that rivaled losing the Cup. Which was absolutely asinine.

He ran a hand over his hair, closed his eyes, and whispered, "*Fuck.*"

# 6

Faith walked the store from back to front, making sure all the aisles were clear, then continued to the door, key in hand. Another long, busy day down on the sales floor. Now came her after-hours work. Pricing, stocking, paying bills, placing orders. Then it started all over again in the morning.

But what kept running through her mind? *Grant didn't come in today.*

She refocused on work, approaching the front door. "I feel like an exhausted hamster."

Sliding her key into the lock, Faith clicked the dead bolt closed. Then she shut her eyes, dropped her forehead against the glass, and sighed.

Her cell rang. Without lifting her head, she pulled it from her back pocket and looked at the screen.

Taylor.

She answered with an upbeat "Hey."

"You sound tired. Rough day?"

"Wow, and I even tried to sound chipper."

"Then never mind—"

"Never mind what?"

"I was going to ask if you could get Caleb from practice. One of my interviews pushed our Skype meeting back an hour. But I'll just tell her—"

"It's fine. I can get him. Kinda late, isn't it?"

"He said the high school practice ran long. They had to wait for the rink. Sounded like Grant worked the high school boys hard today."

*"I talk as dirty as I fight, and I fuck as hard as I play."*

Just remembering Grant's words sent a shiver through her body. And, like striking a match, her sex burned. She hadn't slept at all last night, tortured with guilt over leading him on, shame that she didn't have the courage to step out of her safe little box, and loneliness when she realized that she could have had a warm, sexy man beside her all night.

"Speaking of Grant, what's new with your Hockey Hottie?"

Faith rolled her eyes. "He's not mine, and nothing's new. He didn't even come in today. I told you he'd bail when he figured out I wouldn't jump in bed with him."

"His loss. I have to say, I'm disappointed. After seeing how well he handled that high school team and all those notorious troublemakers, I had higher expectations for him."

Faith didn't blame the guy. It was no fun to want someone and not be wanted back—she'd learned that with Dillon. No fun to physically want someone and go without—she'd learned that last night.

She cleared her throat. "I'll take Caleb through the Dairy Queen drive-through on the way home."

"Are you sure? You should probably just fall into bed."

Fall into bed—alone. Again.

Faith laughed, but she felt hollow. "Like that's going to happen. I have lots of work still ahead of me. I'll grab dinner while I'm there."

"Please tell me it's going to be something other than ice cream."

"No promises."

Taylor groaned, but said, "Thanks, I owe you."

"Good. Let's get started on this video thing." Anything to distract herself from Grant.

Taylor sighed. "Yeah. Okay."

Faith knew then that her hopes for that particular revenue stream was going to have to be put on hold. Taylor had her hands full with her business and Caleb. "Don't worry about that now. I'll drop Caleb home in half an hour."

She disconnected, grabbed the keys to her father's ancient Ford F-150 from the cash register and bundled up to head outside. In the storage-shed-slash-garage out back, Faith climbed into the cab and turned the key.

The old motor chugged, chugged, chugged, and died. She hadn't used this thing in over a week, and every time she did, she always said a prayer that it would start for her. "Come on, baby. Caleb's waiting."

On the third try, the engine revved, and Faith breathed easier. The drive to the outdoor arena was short, and she could see the lights glowing in the darkness long before she approached. But when she turned into the parking lot, she found it empty—except for one black Range Rover.

Her stomach lifted, twisted, then fell.

She parked a couple of spots away from Grant's SUV and looked past the lot to the rink, where only two figures remained on the ice. Grant and Caleb. In fact, they were the only two people anywhere. The rink was deserted except for the two of them.

Faith shut down the engine but stayed in the truck, watching the two skate. She cracked the window to catch their voices carrying on the quiet night, and Grant's low timbre filled her gut with longing.

She tapped out a text message to Taylor. *Did you set this up?*

On the ice, an orange traffic cone sat at one end in front of the goal. Grant picked up two more cones and spaced them out in the middle of the ice, then added another at the opposite end, mirroring the first. Caleb collected a pile of hockey sticks in his arms and skated them out to Grant, where he laid them perpendicular to the length of the rink. It looked like a mini obstacle course. Caleb skated to the opposite end of the rink, while Grant placed a hockey stick across the two cones in the center all while talking to Caleb. Faith couldn't hear what he was saying, but Caleb was rapt and kept nodding his head. And Grant used his hands and body to explain whatever he was talking about. Then he nodded, Caleb imitated him, and Grant patted Caleb's helmet, a hockey-approved show of affection.

Emotion welled in her chest, making it feel tight.

Grant *was* a good guy. If he was like his brothers, he would have been out at the bar every night, not fixing up his parents' guesthouse. He would have been sleeping around with any number of willing single women in town, not dogging her just to be rejected. And he certainly didn't have to be spending extra time on the ice tonight for Caleb.

Her phone buzzed with Taylor's response. *What do you mean? Are you getting paranoid?*

Faith laughed and typed, *Did you buy extra training for Caleb?*

*I don't know what you're talking about. I'd call you, but I have the woman on Skype.*

Faith smiled. *Never mind.*

On the ice, Grant took a hockey stick from Caleb and started through the course in super slow-motion while talking to the boy where he skated alongside, watching and nodding. Grant circled the first cone and glided toward the pair he'd placed at the center of the ice. He picked up speed, and for a moment, Faith thought he was going to jump the stick lying atop the two cones. What terrified her was having Caleb attempt that jump.

Faith reached for the handle, but before she even got the door open, Grant dropped to the ice on his belly instead, sliding underneath the stick and between the cones like he was stealing home base. Caleb was beside himself with laughter but kept watching as Grant picked himself up, skated toward the ladder of sticks he'd placed in front of the other cone, and ran over them, tapping down the tip of his skate blade between each pair of sticks. At the end of the ladder, he skated toward the final cone and stopped sideways, spraying ice over the neon cone.

"Got it?" she heard Grant ask.

She didn't hear Caleb's reply, but he nodded. And Grant started back at the top, skating through the course a little faster, talking it all the way through. And Faith found herself just as rapt as Caleb, loving Grant's fluidity, his agility, his athleticism.

At the end, he sprayed the cone again. And Caleb laughed.

"Do it again," Caleb said. "This time full speed. Like you'd do it in your practice."

Faith grinned, rested her elbow on the window ledge, and leaned her head against her fist.

Grant complied with Caleb's request, but he built up some speed first, rotating his right shoulder a couple of times before he headed for the first cone. The intensity of the approach made Faith's breath catch. Then he was flying through the moves, and before she had time to process his skill, he was done, spraying the cone with ice until the neon orange was invisible.

Caleb laughed and clapped gloved hands. Grant gestured to the opposite cone. "Your turn."

Faith watched as Caleb took the course again and again under Grant's watchful eye. She watched as Caleb faltered and fell. Kicked the cones out of place and sent the hockey sticks flying. And each time, Grant patiently replaced all the props and encouraged him to go again. Once, when Caleb hit the ice hard enough for Faith to wince, Grant skated to him, braced himself on his knees and talked to Caleb but didn't help him up. Faith knew that was to show support but also to teach Caleb he had to get up on his own.

And the first time Caleb made it through the drill successfully, no displaced equipment, a nice heavy spray on the cone, her heart all but burst with excitement for him. The kid who struggled endlessly with anything athletic had finally mastered a drill. He and Grant shared a high five before Caleb went back to the top of the ice and continued running the exercise, just because he wanted to.

Faith pushed from the truck and started toward the rink. When the truck's door closed, Grant looked over.

"Hey." His tone held a little what-are-you-doing-here, and his smile seemed a little tight.

Faith didn't blame him, but it did take a little thrill out of her excitement. "Hey. Taylor asked me to pick up Caleb."

Caleb sprayed the cone, then yelled, "Wah-hoo! Aunt Faith, did you see that?"

"I've seen it all fifty-seven times," she told him. "I've been watching."

"If I do it again, can you video it for Mom?"

Grant glided toward Faith as she pulled her phone from her pocket. "You bet."

Caleb made his way across the rink, giving Faith time with Grant. "It's really sweet of you to take time with him. He—"

"Struggles," Grant said. "I know. He just needs some one-on-one. He picks up the moves fast when he's focused."

"He's a really smart kid."

"That's good." Grant grinned and rested his hip on the railing, looking out into the rink. "I know it doesn't seem like it, but you've got to be pretty sharp in hockey. Everything moves so fast. If you don't think faster..." He shrugged.

Beside him, Faith pressed her hands to the worn wood and

leaned forward to see the whole rink. "I missed seeing you today."

"I finished grouting the shower tile," he said. "And then I found mold under the sink."

She groaned. "Oh no."

He shrugged and smiled. "Just means I get to come in tomorrow."

She took a deep breath and pushed through her nerves to say, "I'm really sorry about yesterday." She forced herself to meet his eyes. "I—"

"Aunt Faith?" Caleb yelled. "Are you ready?"

Grant called, "Take a practice run."

Faith laughed.

"I've already taken fifty-seven practice runs, according to Aunt Faith."

"Take fifty-eight," Grant told him. Then he grinned at Faith. "He's a really good sport. Half the high school team would have dropped like flies by now. He has a future in high school hockey if his tenacity holds."

"That news will thrill his mom."

Grant nodded. "I'm sorry about yesterday too. I pushed too hard. I forget not everyone is as intense as I am." He held her gaze, but the passion from the day before was absent, and Faith discovered she missed it. "But I'm not sorry about what happened. I wanted to kiss you from the first day."

"I'm re-ady," Caleb sang, skating restless circles. "Whenever you are..."

Faith laughed, and the uncomfortable tension she'd been feeling since Grant walked out of the store yesterday finally ebbed a little. She lifted her phone toward the rink. "Okay."

She tapped <Record> and followed Caleb through the drill. When Caleb sprayed the cone, Grant put his fingers in his mouth and whistled. Faith cringed and covered the ear closest to him.

"Oh," he said, laughing. "Sorry."

She shoved his shoulder. "Are not."

He caught her wrist, and held it. Their eyes met, and there was no freaking way she could deny the pull between them. But Grant didn't push it. He loosened his grip and slid his hand over hers, then yelled at Caleb, "Clean up, kid."

Without one word of protest, Caleb started picking up cones and sticks, dragging them to the bench and tucking them away in equipment bags.

Grant looked down at their hands and threaded their fingers but didn't speak, and the moment felt unnervingly intimate.

"I wish he couldn't see us," Grant murmured. "Because I'd kiss you again."

All the feelings from the day before rushed in, mixing with new nerves, and she breathed, "Yeah."

Grant chuckled, squeezed her hand, and met her eyes. His were relaxed, but a spark was missing, and that made her sad. He lifted a hand, swept a piece of hair off her cheek, then tucked it behind her ear in a gesture so tender, it flipped Faith's heart. "Headed home?"

Her stomach did that squeezing thing again, but this time she couldn't tell if it was fear or excitement. "No. I have to take him back first. And I told Taylor I was going to take him through the Dairy Queen drive-through, which means she'll be expecting her regular."

He grinned. "What's her regular?"

"Oreo."

"And what's your regular?" he asked.

She shook her head. "I don't have one. I try something new every time I go."

He lifted his brows. "Really."

"Yeah, I know. I'm reckless like that."

He chuckled, opened his fingers, and slid his hand against hers. "I like reckless."

She nodded. "I figured. What's your regular?"

He lifted his gaze to the rink. "I'd like to taste Faith Nicholas again. I didn't get enough the first time to tell if it was my flavor or not."

Her whole body erupted in a burst of tingling heat.

She hummed a laugh, and before she could think of a witty comeback, Caleb streaked across the ice, shoes and hockey stick in one hand, blade guards in the other. "I'm ready to go. Wait till Mom sees me."

Grant released her hand and pushed off the wall, putting space between them as Caleb jumped and turned, planting his ass on the ledge. He slid on his guards, then changed from skates to tennis shoes while talking nonstop about practice.

Grant egged him on but kept looking at Faith as he shifted restlessly on his own skates. While Faith's mind was spinning a mile a minute—ask him to come over, or leave it relaxed between them? Go for it, or let things end on a good note? Was she ready to jump back into the deep end? Should she do it with this guy?

The flutter in her belly told her she was pretty sure he'd drag her under and drown her without ever realizing. But then she wondered if she were underestimating herself. Underestimating him.

"Aunt Faith." Caleb's frustrated voice dragged her gaze from Grant's grin.

"What?"

Caleb was already standing outside the rink, skates in hand, arms out.

"Hey." She frowned at him. "Lose the attitude, or you can walk home, buddy."

He deflated. "Okay. I'm sorry."

"What do you say to Grant? And think before you answer."

Her warning tone registered, but he still answered immediately. "That was the best practice ever, Mr. Saber."

"Grant," he said, chuckling, then grimaced. "No Mr. Saber."

"Sorry. But seriously, I've never had so much fun playing hockey before. Thank you."

"I'm glad. Thanks for giving it your all."

"Okay," Faith said, reluctant to walk away from Grant. But she tugged on the hood of Caleb's sweatshirt, teasingly dragging him right, then left, then right again until he was laughing. "I guess we can go to Dairy Queen on the way home."

Caleb jumped and fisted his hand. "*Yes.*" And he ran to the truck, yelling, "Thanks for the extra practice, Mr... Grant."

"He's a good kid," Grant said, waving to Caleb before he jumped in the truck.

Faith walked backward a few feet. "And you're a good man, Grant Saber."

Grant dropped his hand and looked at her for a long, deer-in-the-headlights moment before a grin split his face.

Faith's heart tripped again. And to keep herself from falling over her feet, Faith turned and jogged the rest of the way to the truck. When she backed out of the parking space, she glanced over at the ice and found Grant sprinting from one end of the rink to the other, a puck at the blade of his stick, swooshing around corners, taking sharp turns, and speeding back the other direction.

She paused a moment to watch, mesmerized by his speed and intensity. The sight made her body tighten in ways she hadn't felt in so long, she wasn't sure she'd ever felt quite like this. "I need to start watching more hockey."

"I told you that when I was, like, five."

Faith reached across the bench seat and stuck a finger in Caleb's ticklish ribs. He burst into giggles that warmed Faith's heart. "Shush, monkey. Be nice, or no Blizzard for you."

She only half listened to Caleb's constant chatter on the

drive, her mind spinning around how quickly her desire for Grant had ramped up over the span of a week. She'd been single for eight years now. During that time, she'd made a lot of male friends and been asked out dozens of times. But she'd only met maybe a handful of guys who'd tempted her to date again, and not one who'd made her want to jump into bed with him.

Yet here she was, losing sleep over Grant. And it wasn't just because of his looks. Sure, that was a benefit, but what had captured her attention was his confidence and wit. What had deepened her interest was all she'd learned about him during his daily visits to the store. The way he stopped to talk to locals. His easy nature and quick laughter. And the way he continued to fix up his parents' home even when their relationship was strained. How he'd stayed in town even after a blowup with them to honor his commitment to Dwayne and support a team that had once been his team.

"I couldn't believe it when he told me he'd been bullied in school." Caleb's comment broke into Faith's thoughts.

She glanced at him. "What?"

"Mr. Saber. He told me that he was really unpopular as a kid. He got picked on a lot, like me."

Her brows shot up, and a grin turned her mouth. He'd probably made that up to make Caleb feel better. "Really?"

"Uh-huh. He was super skinny and had really bad pimples, you know? What do you call that?"

"Acne?"

"Yeah, that. He said kids called him names for a long time. You know, the way they call me nerd and dweeb and stuff."

"Oh yeah?" Faith's brows pulled together. She was having a hard time picturing that.

"Yeah. Told me that people only started to respect him when he got good at hockey. Said I didn't have to choose hockey, but that finding something that I'm really good at will make other people respect me. And over time, people would stop teasing me. He said I shouldn't be afraid to be me. That too many people spend too much time trying to fit in when they should be trying to stand out and be their own personal best."

That sting of warmth she'd had earlier filled her again, and she smiled pulling into the Dairy Queen drive-through.

Grant Saber just kept surprising her.

Faith was still thinking about Grant long after she'd dropped Caleb off at home and returned to the store to finish up her day by stocking shelves. Thinking about his kiss as she started toward the basement where dozens of delivery boxes awaited her. Thinking about his words that still created a shiver in her gut and settled heat between her legs.

*"I talk as dirty as I fight, and I fuck as hard as I play."*

She wondered what it would be like to have a man like Grant Saber, with all his confidence and skill, talk dirty to her. Wondered what it would be like to be fucked hard. Hell, fucked period. She'd never approached sex that way. Dillon had been her first and last. And she'd been in love with him. Had believed she'd marry him.

As she unloaded the last box, Faith came to the realization that nothing in life was a sure thing—except death. And that by trying so hard to hold on to the store, she was letting life pass her by. A big chunk of which she'd already missed out on. It didn't matter whether Grant wanted one night or even one hour, because the truth was, with her life so unstable, Faith didn't have much more to offer.

Gathering the last box of nuts, bolts, and screws, she started upstairs to fill the shelves.

"Tomorrow," she told herself, "I'm going to ask him out. Tomorrow, when he comes in, I'm going to see if he wants to go to dinner. I'm going to be honest with him, and if he's still interested, then..." She paused on the stairs. "Then what?"

The thought of having sex with him electrified her blood.

Just kissing him had knocked her completely off-balance. What would she do when she was naked? When *he* was naked? Or when his hands roamed her body? When his mouth ventured beyond her lips? When he moved between her legs and pushed inside her.

A wave of want crashed, making her so dizzy, she had to put a hand against the wall to steady herself. "God," she said, the word shaky with excitement, anticipation... Fear. She forced her feet to move again. "He's so out of my stratosphere. It's probably time to check into some video education tonigh—"

*Psssssssss...*

Faith's feet froze on the stairs. Her ears perked to the new high-pressured hiss coming from somewhere adjacent to the storage room. It was the kind of sound that prickled the skin on the back of her neck with alarm.

She turned and started back to the basement, her mind searching for the cause. The explosion shocked her, and Faith tripped over her own feet. She let out a cry just before she hit the cement stairs. Pain cracked through her butt and back, stealing her breath. The box she'd been carrying slammed against the wall, then the floor, spraying silver screws like confetti.

Faith used her hands to slow her momentum and brace herself once she'd come to a stop. But several moments passed before she could gain control over her breathing to ease the pain that stabbed along her back and butt.

When it finally eased enough to let her draw full breaths, her other senses came back, and a new horror flooded in—the sound of

# 7

Gushing water.

Grant had pushed everything too far this week—his frustration with his parents, his desire for Faith, and the limits of his own body. And he was paying for all of them.

He let the hot water pulse from the new showerhead over his right shoulder, glad he'd gone for the more expensive model and all the massage features. After this, he'd stretch, then pack it with ice. Add a little ibuprofen and a good night's sleep, and he'd be fine tomorrow.

But sleep wouldn't come easily. All he had to do was remember the feel of Faith's warm mouth under his. The gentle way she'd stroked his tongue when she'd found the nerve. The way she felt against him. And, God, the sounds she made when he kissed her...

All his blood flowed south again. His groin tightened. His cock hardened.

"Fuck." Grant opened his eyes to his hard-on and sighed. It was going to be another long night.

He hit the controls, pulled the towel from the shower door, and pressed it against his face. His brothers would be here tomorrow. Initially, that would buffer him from his parents. But Grant suspected that Patrick and Shawn would become as big a source of stress and frustration as his parents were. And even after all these years, that really disappointed him.

As he dried off, he thought of Faith and her relationship with her father and Caleb, a boy she wasn't even related to by blood. They were loving, nurturing, and kind. Because Faith was loving, nurturing, and kind. And it made Grant wonder if it was time to add that kind of happiness and warmth into his own life.

But that was extremely hard to do in his line of work with a grueling game and practice schedule that included travel, charity and team events. When he was surrounded by women who were more interested in what kind of fame or finances he brought to the table instead of what kind of man he was.

*"And you're a good man, Grant Saber."*

Faith's words made him smile. He didn't feel like he deserved them, but he wanted to deserve them. Now he wished he had more time to earn them with her.

His phone chimed with a call. Grant closed his eyes, sighed, and picked up the phone. He didn't recognize the number, just that it was local, and hoped Bobby Lowry was calling to get together. It would be good to see him and it might help keep Grant's mind off Faith.

"Hello," he answered, scrubbing his hair with the towel.

"Hey, Grant?"

He recognized Faith's voice immediately, which threw him completely off axis. "Faith?"

She huffed a tired laugh. "Who were you expecting? How many women do you have calling you at this hour?" He grinned at her quick sarcasm, but she didn't sound quite right. "Hold on. Never mind. Don't answer that."

"Are you out of breath? Or just tipsy?" Lowering his voice, he teased, "Did you get into the Jangle Punch again?"

"Yeah, that's it." There was definitely something off in her voice. "If you get here soon, I might still have some to share with you."

He didn't get a chance to ask if she was serious, because the line went dead. Grant pulled his phone from his ear and stared at it. Then shrugged. Jangle Punch or no Jangle Punch, there was nowhere he'd rather be than with Faith. Annoyed or not.

He reached for the bathroom door.

A knock came from the entry to the guesthouse, followed by, "Grant?"

He cringed at the sound of his mother's voice and leaned on the door handle. "Yeah, Mom. Taking a shower."

"Sorry, honey. I wanted to tell you that Patrick came in early. And Shawn's going to be delayed. Do you think you could come up to the house for a drink before you turn in? Patrick's interested in the landscaping barrier you put in the planting beds out front. Says he'd like to use it at his house and had some questions."

"Shit," he whispered, then said, "Actually, I promised Dwayne I'd meet him to talk about some team strategy tonight. Can you tell Patrick I'll catch him tomorrow?"

"Oh." She sounded disappointed, and Grant braced for her incensed anger. "All right."

When she didn't say more, Grant said, "Thanks."

"Sure." Pause. "Honey, I just wanted to tell you that your dad and I really appreciate all you've done around the house this past week, and despite our rough start, it's been so nice having you home."

He rubbed his face, so not in the mood to deal with this. Nor did he know what to say. Based on years of experience, he wasn't ready to jump into expectations. "Thanks, Mom. I'm glad."

"Tomorrow maybe we can sit down with your schedule and see when we can all make it to one of your games."

He dropped his hand, lifted his head, and stared at the door. "Really?"

Okay, that wasn't what he'd meant to say out loud, but...*really*?

"Yes, really. You know, your dad's been under a lot of stress at work. Normally he's not so...angry." She paused. "Well, say hello to Dwayne for us. We'll talk to you in the morning."

When the door closed, Grant shook his head and muttered, "Who was that, and what did she do with my mother?"

But he wondered only for a second, because he had someone very special waiting for him.

Grant splashed on a little cologne and dressed in jeans and a tee, and was out the door in two minutes flat. He shrugged into his parka on the jog to his SUV sitting in the drive and headed toward town.

With edgy alternative rock shaking the car and his mind spiraling through what-ifs over Faith's phone call—specifically, what if she'd called to tell him she wanted him and just couldn't find the words?—Grant was primed and pumped when he took the steps to the store two at a time and found the front door open. He stepped into the darkened store to the familiar tinkle of a bell and the rasp of his own quick breath.

He was just about to call for her when Faith's voice floated up from the basement. "I'm down here."

Grant frowned. "And...what are you doing down there?"

At the bottom of the stairs, he found three feet of water covering the concrete floor and Faith dressed in the same clothes she'd been wearing at the rink—only now she was soaking wet.

She reached high to add a box to the top of a shelving unit and glanced over her shoulder. "Well, hello, Mr. Saber."

All his excitement evaporated, and his shoulders sank. He hooked his thumbs through the belt loops of his jeans and tilted his head. A pipe had obviously broken, and it hadn't happened in the last fifteen minutes.

"I'm guessing this means there's no Jangle Punch awaiting me," he said.

"And I'm guessing that's not all you thought would be awaiting you." She gave him a smile and a shrug. "But you might still get Jangle Punch out of this if you play your cards right. Yuletide is just a block away. Unfortunately, I have to get this worked out before I can go anywhere." She gave him an overly sweet smile and a dramatic bat of her lashes. "If you'd like to help, it might go faster."

Grant heaved a sigh and rubbed his eyes.

"Don't act all put out," she said, amused by his disappointment. "You live three minutes away, and I have other people I can call to help. The door is right behind you."

"So…I was your first call?"

She crossed her arms. "You were."

That mollified him. Grant shrugged out of his parka. "Why'd the pipe break?"

"I don't know. Everything's insulated. Might have just suffered one expansion too many. I got the water turned off pretty fast, and I have everything I need to replace the pipe, but there's one fitting that's on so tight, I can't loosen it. I've called three plumbers, none of whom are available for a minimum of three days—so much for emergency plumbers, right?"

He grinned at her. "You said I was your first call."

She leveled a heavy-lidded look on him. "The pipe blew right at an elbow, and to fix it, I've got to get the elbow off. But it's crimped down so tight, I can't move it. If you can just loosen the fitting for me, I can do the rest myself."

Of course she could. "You can do just about everything yourself, can't you?"

"As a matter of fact," she said, her smile way too sweet, her expression way too innocent. "But hey, if you want to fix my pipes while you're here, Mr. Fix-it, I'm not going to stop you."

"As a matter of fact," he echoed her, "I would, but this wasn't what I had in mind." Her face pinked up, her gaze lowered, and she pushed her hands into her back pockets. The move made Grant focus on her chest. Made him realize her T-shirt was white. White and wet. And the curves it clung to made everything inside Grant ache.

"I figured." Faith sloshed through the water to the bottom of the stairs, rummaged in a toolbox there, and pulled out a flashlight and a pair of pliers. She handed them to Grant. "Let's talk about that when you're done."

Hope bloomed through him. He grinned and took the tools. "That's way better than Jangle punch."

He waded into the water in search of the damaged pipe, forcing his mind to getting this pipe fixed. He clamped the end of the small flashlight between his teeth, then gripped the fitting with the pliers and twisted—a movement his shoulder didn't like much. The metal spun a little but didn't loosen.

"Why don't you have a girlfriend back in DC?" Her question came out of nowhere and raised warning flags in Grant's head. Faith was girlfriend material; it only made sense that she'd ask. It also only seemed fair that he was honest with her, even if it meant killing any chance he had of sleeping with her.

He pulled the flashlight from his mouth. "Because my life makes anything more difficult." He glanced at her and she met his gaze, open and nonjudgmental. "And because that's how I like it."

When she gave a nod, he went back to work on the fitting —unsuccessfully.

He paused again. "I need another pair of pliers."

Metal clanged against metal as she searched for more tools. Grant couldn't keep himself from admiring the way her jeans pulled taut over her ass. "Why don't you have a boyfriend?"

"Because I was taking care of my dad and running the store. I haven't had time for anything else." She offered him another pair of pliers. "Here."

He took them, humbled again. She had to be one of the most unselfish people he'd ever met. And she really didn't have anyone to fall back on.

"What?"

Her question made him realize he was still staring at her. Grant shook his head and turned back to the pipe. "I was just thinking what a stupid prick Dillon was to let you go. Definitely his loss."

She remained quiet a minute, and Grant rolled the pain from his shoulder.

"Well," she finally said, her voice softer, "when you're in the spotlight like he was, with everyone telling you how fantastic you are all the time, I guess your feet start to lift off the ground. And when you feel a little higher and mightier than others, I guess your needs somehow seem a lot more important."

Those words hit their mark, and Grant's stomach dropped. He paused and glanced at her over his shoulder. "You're right," he said, adequately humbled. "That does happen. It's good to be reminded we're mortal every once in a while."

He replaced the light between his teeth, positioned the pliers, and used all his strength to twist. Three tries later, the fitting loosened and the elbow separated from the vertical pipe.

Pain burned through Grant's shoulder joint, and he swore and rolled out the sting.

"Are you okay?" she asked.

"I'm just sore. Between the fixes at the house and practices, I've used it a little too much this week."

After loosening the attached piece, he sloshed toward her with the bad length of copper.

Faith's body loosened in relief, and she smiled. "Oh, thank you so much."

"You're welcome." He set all the tools and the pipe on shelves nearby. "Are you sure you can get the rest, or do you want me to help while I'm here?"

"No, no. I can get it."

He gave her a nod and sloshed toward the stairs. "Well, it's late. I should let you—"

Something tugged on his shirt. When he turned to see what he'd snagged it on, Grant found Faith's arm extended, reaching for a fistful of his tee.

"Thank you." She released his shirt and stepped back. "I really appreciate you coming over. This...freaked me out a little. I haven't had anything big go wrong since my dad died."

His heart twisted. "I can't imagine how hard it must be to handle all this on your own."

"Most days..." She shrugged. "I manage. But while you're here..." She looked frazzled and vulnerable and so fucking beautiful with her bright eyes and flushed cheeks. "I was going to ask you tomorrow when you came by, but you're here now, so..." She took a breath. "Do you want to go to dinner maybe? Or something? On a night when, you know, you don't have practice?"

A zing of excitement coursed along his nerves, but he tamped it down. Grant planted his hands on his hips and lifted his brows. "Did you just ask me out?"

She dragged her lower lip between her teeth, fidgeted with the hem of her tee, and smiled a little. "Um, yeah."

He grinned. "Have you ever done that before?"

She laughed. "No. Pretty obvious, huh?"

Grant pressed one hand to the cement wall and exhaled. "Is that what you really want, Faith? Dinner at a restaurant?"

She worked her lower lip some more. Then shook her head.

"What do you really want?"

She held his gaze but didn't answer for a long time. And Grant didn't pressure her, because he could see her working it out in her head. And because he knew this was a big step for her.

"You." The word came out as a half whisper. She cleared her throat and said, "You. I want you. I want..." She exhaled heavily and shook her head. "I want to know what it's like to be with you. With a man like you. Part of me wants just an hour. Part of me wants all night. I'm willing to take whatever works for you. I don't...expect...anything more. I know you're only going to be here a short time, and..."

She let her eyes close and all the air leak from her lungs as if the words exhausted her and she couldn't bring herself to say more.

Grant was strung tight. Walking in, he'd known what he'd wanted—to corrupt a sweet country girl into a hot fling. Now... he still wanted that. But he wanted something else too. He just wasn't sure what.

She was four feet away, and he needed her closer. Much closer. "Come here."

She lifted her gaze to his, her eyes clear but confused. And she looked so fucking innocent right now Grant couldn't believe how badly he wanted her. Couldn't believe how hot she made him, looking like a drowned mouse. Or how those big blue eyes cut into him.

When she didn't move he said, "Come. Here."

She waded through the water and stopped six inches away.

He lifted his hand, stroked her cheek, and cupped her jaw, with a murmured "You are so fucking beautiful."

Her lashes fluttered and closed. She leaned her head into his hand. And fire consumed Grant's body. He'd always thought he preferred spunky, take-charge women. Women he didn't have to work to get or work to please. But he couldn't remember ever being this charged by a woman either.

"Tell me what you want, Faith."

She opened her eyes, took the last step to close the distance between them, and reached out, taking handfuls of his tee into her fingers to twist. "I want you to take charge."

His mind flashed back to their moment in the back room, and heat flooded his groin. His heart picked up speed.

"And I want you to do it your way," she said, dropping his shirt and sliding her hands underneath, across his skin. Her cold fingers made him flinch but still created a sizzle in his body. One that cut straight to his cock. She curved her arms around his waist, pressed that awesome little body against his, and looked up at him with those big, trusting eyes. "I want you to talk as dirty as you fight, and I want you to fuck me as hard as you play."

Another jolt of lust slammed through his body and hardened his cock. But he narrowed his eyes and brought his hand under her jaw to grip her face hard enough to make her draw a breath. "You don't know what you're asking for."

"I want to know." Fire burned in her eyes, and her fingers dug into his back. "I want you to show me."

God, he wanted to show her. Wanted to show her every carnal detail involved in fucking. But... "Baby, I'm pretty sure my definition of fucking and yours are on alternate planes of reality."

Her eyes darkened, and her jaw tightened. One of her hands came around and pushed between them to work open the button on his jeans, then slide the zipper, all while she never took her gaze off his. "Then bring me over to the dark side. Or is your schedule too booked up to give a girl a few fucking lessons?"

He released her jaw and pressed his fingers to her lips. "Stop saying that. It's... God, it makes me insane."

Her small hand slipped into his jeans and beneath his boxers, then closed around his cock. The combination of cold and pressure shocked a jerk through his whole body, and he swore. Then she opened her lips and took his fingers into her warm mouth.

All the sensations overloaded his circuits.

He pulled his hand from her mouth, wrapped it around the back of her neck, and dragged her mouth to his. With the other arm at her waist, he drew her against him, tasted her deeply, and groaned with all the frustration and need that had built up over the last week. She kissed him back far more openly, more hungrily than she had the first time, and the feel of her wanting him so passionately blew a fuse.

Grant lifted her off her feet. The move dragged her hand from his jeans, and she broke the kiss on a gasp.

"Grant, your shoulder. Put me down."

A sweet pang tugged inside him. No one but Dwayne had asked about his shoulder, not even his parents. He found her neck with his lips as he climbed the stairs and dragged her up his body until she wrapped her legs around his hips. "My shoulder can handle you."

She was cold and wet and sent shivers over his entire body.

"You're cold," he muttered against her skin.

"Only on the outside."

When he reached the top of the stairs, Grant stepped over his jacket and paused to drag at her tee, pulling it off over her head. He dropped it in a soggy clump on the floor. She wore a white bra with lace edges. Her breasts were round and plump, and he trailed his fingers over the curve of one, loving the way her puckered nipples stood out against the silk.

"Oh, man, I was so wrong." He slid his fingers up her chest, her neck, and around to her nape again before meeting her eyes. "Fast isn't going to work with you. I'm definitely going to have to take my time."

# 8

Faith couldn't seem to pull in enough air. Or maybe she'd lost the blood supply to her brain. All she knew was her head felt light and dizzy, and she couldn't think straight with Grant's erection pressed between her legs. Even with two layers of denim between them, his heat burned through, and she was dying to feel him more intimately.

With Grant carrying her, one hand supporting the middle of her back, he crossed the sales floor at a snail's pace, preoccupied with stroking her breasts and teasing her nipples. This wasn't what she'd expected. Faith had expected a wild flurry of wall-banging, animalistic sex once she'd told him what she wanted. But as she gripped his tee to keep from falling backward, he was focused on her breasts as if they were the Holy Grail or held the secret to the universe or something. And every slide of his finger over her nipple felt like a stroke between her legs and made her wriggle and moan.

"Sensitive," he murmured, slipping his finger beneath the clasp between her breasts and flicking it open.

The silk fell aside, exposing her. A sudden sense of vulnerability made her shiver. He hummed with pleasure at the sight and cupped one breast with his whole hand, squeezing and stroking. Brushing her nipple with his thumb. The touch was like lightning through her core, darting straight between her legs and pushing a whimper from her throat. By the time he reached the door leading to her apartment on the opposite side of the store, Faith thought she might be on the edge of orgasm. All she could think about was the ache between her legs and the way it pulsed as quickly as her heartbeat. Knew how badly she needed to sate the need clawing deep at her core.

But instead of opening her door and taking her upstairs, Grant lifted her to the edge of the shipping counter along the back wall. Shoving tape and scissors and pens aside, he laid her back across the wide, solid wooden surface that had been a fixture at the store as long as she'd been alive. Faith had to prop herself up with her elbows to keep her head from hitting the wall, which rendered her hands useless. And when Grant straightened and stared down at her, raking her with those hot, hungry eyes, she was sure she'd never felt more exposed, more helpless, more excited, or more beautiful.

"Take me upstairs," she told him, her voice breathy with the effort. "The door's unlocked."

"Not yet." He put both hands at her waist, slid them up to her breasts, and cupped. Molded. Stroked.

"Grant, I want—"

He met her eyes and brushed both nipples with all five fingers of each hand. The shock of pleasure tingled over the flesh of her breasts first, followed a millisecond later by deep, penetrating pleasure. Pleasure that transferred directly between her legs and made her lift her hips to rub against him while a low, hungry sound vibrated in her throat and her eyes fell closed.

"What—exactly—do you want, Faith?" His voice was low, raspy, and serious, with an edge of darkness. "Because I thought I knew what I wanted when I came. And since I've touched you, that's totally changed."

She forced her eyes open and pushed up on her hands. "What...do you mean?"

"I came to hook up with a sexy country girl who knows her own mind and doesn't take any shit."

His fingertips brushed the opposite direction, zapping another lightning strike of pleasure through her. She whimpered, and her head fell back, just missing the wall. "Ah...God..."

A growl rolled from his throat, and he closed his hands on her breasts hard, making Faith wince.

"But just getting this tiny glimpse of your sexy side makes me want all kinds of other things. Things I haven't wanted in years. Things I may never have wanted. Things that turn me inside out."

He took one nipple between his fingers, pinched hard, shooting a spike of lust through her chest and sex at the same time. Then he rolled it gently, rubbing away the pain and stroking excitement back into her body until all Faith could do was arch and whimper and moan. "Grant."

He pressed his lips to her temple and kissed her. "So tell me what you want, Faith," he murmured, his rich, husky voice tingling down her neck and over her shoulder. "What you *really* want. So I know where my boundaries are."

Boundaries? She didn't know anything about boundaries in sex.

"I...don't know what...you mean." She was panting and aching, and she really just wanted to feel him inside her.

He lifted his head, pressed one hand to the table and met her gaze deliberately. "I mean you make me *fucking insane*," he said from behind clenched teeth. "I mean that every little flicker of your pleasure is like a hit of my favorite drug and drives me like a fucking addict." He brushed her nipple, and she shivered. Then he pinched it, and she gasped. Rolled it and she moaned. "I want to do whatever it takes to get those sounds out of your mouth. Whatever it takes to keep that drugged look in your eyes. Whatever it takes to get you as addicted to me as I am to you right now."

"Yes," she said, breathless, and leaned into one arm to lift the other and wrap it around his head. "Yes, I want that."

"Even if that means letting me have control? *Complete* control?" He paused, and a shiver rattled through her chest. "Say yes, Faith."

He made it seem so simple. And she heard herself say, "Yes."

He pulled back and searched her eyes. His were fiery and intense. "Even if that means giving me *complete*, *unrestricted* access to *every inch* of your body?" Another pause, then a deliberate "Say yes, Faith."

A heat wave washed her sex. Tension pulled her muscles taut. Still, her lips formed the word, "Yes."

His hand closed in her hair and pulled her head back. A sting radiated through her scalp. A cry of surprise rolled from her throat, and she fell back onto her elbows. Grant leaned farther over her, pushing his erection harder against the need throbbing angrily between her legs.

"You're going to let me fuck you any way I want? Any time I want?"

She couldn't think straight, but the way she felt right now, with him pressed against her sex even with clothes on... That was a big affirmative. "*Yes.*"

He used the hand braced on the table to grip her jaw, making him list forward. Making him press into her harder. His gaze darkened, hardened, and heated, but a sliver of panic still lived there. "You're going to let me fuck you with my hands. You're going to let me fuck you with my mouth. You're going to let me fuck you with my cock." He paused. "You're going to let me fuck you with any other random thing I decide will bring you screaming orgasmic pleasure."

Holy hell. Her body was completely wigging out on her. Lust surged through her system, almost too much to handle. "*Please.*"

He tightened his hand on her face and shook her. "Say. Yes. Faith."

"Yes, yes. Please. *Yes.*"

"*Fuck.*" He jerked his hand from her face and fisted her hair again, with an angry "You're supposed to say *no.*"

"Feels so good." She exhaled, trying to control the wild need his dominant behavior pulled out of her. "I want it."

He opened and closed the hand in her hair, restlessly, creating a fresh burn with every clench. Faith moaned and lifted her hips against his. Fire flashed in his eyes, and he rocked against her.

"Yes..." She clasped one of his forearms. The hard muscles flexed and rolled beneath her hand. "Want you so—"

He lowered his head and attacked her mouth. His hips hammered against hers, and the pressure released a shaft of ecstasy through her lower body. Her mouth went slack, and Grant drove his tongue in, found hers and stroked, circled, teased, while his hips rocked and pulsed. He sucked her lips in turn. Scraped them between his teeth until she winced. He ate at her and ate at her while she simply struggled to keep up. While the excitement in her body rose, and her back arched, and the need to find the peak intensified.

And as his own passion rose, his grasp on her hair grew tighter, the burn in her scalp hotter, his thrusts harder. He finally pulled out of the kiss and pressed his forehead to hers. "You like rough..." he panted. "So fucking hot... Never would have guessed..."

Neither would she. But he wasn't the only one feeling a

little insane. She had to be a little crazy to agree to what she'd agreed to.

Grant dipped his head again, but this time focused on her breasts and stroked his tongue across one bud. Liquid heat spread through Faith's chest and her sex at the same time. Her mouth dropped open, her fingers curled into fists, and her eyes rolled back in her head. Then he closed his mouth over her nipple and sucked.

Faith moaned and shivered. "Grant..." she moaned at his temple, "God..."

He scraped his teeth over her nipple, then bit down in teasing pulses while he used his fingers on her other breast. The sensations were wildly excruciating, drawing Faith to the edge of orgasm.

"Take me...upstairs..." she begged.

He pulled his mouth away from her body, turned his head, and kissed her again, stealing her breath. He used the other hand to spread the wetness of his mouth over her breast, teasing her nipple over and over and over, creating a whole new kind of slick friction. His tongue stroked and plunged and spiraled against Faith's until he finally broke for air. But then he went right back to work on her other breast.

Her whimper for relief fell on deaf ears. Faith's vision blurred; her head swam. She'd never known she could want someone so badly. Never guessed a desire so intense lived inside her, but she was wild with need.

"Oh my God..." she said, breathless. "Can't take any more."

"You can," he told her, his tone short and final. "And you will."

Then he teased and tortured her right over the edge into what felt like a mini orgasm. A wholly unsatisfying and superficial orgasm that barely scratched the surface of her need and left her even hungrier than before. The tension drained from her muscles, and Faith slumped back on the wide table, resting her shoulders against the wall while she caught her breath.

But Grant didn't take a break. "That's a good start."

His hands went right for her jeans, popping the button, pulling at the zipper. He tugged them off her legs, fighting and swearing when the wet denim suctioned to her skin. She pushed herself forward long enough to grab a handful of his tee. Then battled with him to give up the cotton until he let her pull it off over his head. And while Faith suffered another heat wave at the sight of all his muscle and bronze skin, Grant focused on her white bikini panties.

All it took was one pass of those big, warm hands over her thighs to rekindle her need. And when his touch passed between her legs and over her sex, her lust spiked. Then his fingers were gone, leaving Faith throbbing again.

Just when she was about to complain, he gripped the low waistband of her panties and curled it around his fingers. He hooked his other hand under one knee and dragged her thighs wide. Faith laid her hands flat on the table for balance. She was in no position to do anything more than watch him study her sex. Watch him pull her panties taut. Watch him work the fabric into the folds until her swollen clit pressed taut against the silk.

"Mmmm," he murmured, running his tongue over his bottom lip. "That is juicy perfection right there."

He playfully jerked on her panties, pulsing the pressure against her clit just enough to make her writhe. The fingers of his free hand slipped underneath the bunched fabric and stroked her opening. Faith drew a sharp breath, and her sex clenched in automatic reaction.

Grant chuckled under his breath, settled his gaze on her face, and watched her reaction as he stroked her and stroked her and stroked her. And fuck, that felt beyond amazing. Faith pushed up to her hands for leverage, then lifted her hips into his touch.

"You like my fingers on you?"

"Yes..." The words came out breathless and completely wanton.

"Do you want them inside you?"

She choked on a sob of desire. "Yes, yes, yes."

He scraped his lower lip between his teeth and pulled his hand from between her legs. Opening his hand toward her, he leaned close and whispered, "Look how wet you are."

Her gaze refocused on his hand and the glistening surface of his fingertips. Then followed the sight right into his mouth. She pulled in a sharp breath, shocked at the raw eroticism. But when Grant closed his lips around his fingers, moaned in pleasure, and closed his eyes in an expression of bliss, lust flooded Faith's body.

She leaned into one hand and reached for his waistband with the other. Grant easily caught her wrist and pressed her hand back to the tabletop, his gaze hot and determined on hers. "No. Hands. While yours stay here"—he released her wrist and brought his hand between her legs—"mine stay here."

And with his eyes on hers, silently demanding she hold his gaze, he circled her opening again, until Faith couldn't hold still anymore. She lifted and rocked toward his touch, making Grant smile, a hot devilish little smile.

"Baby, I hope you don't plan on sleeping tonight. Because I have so many things I want to do to you."

And then he slowly pushed inside her. The sensation stole Faith's breath. She was so absorbed in the feeling of penetration, everything in her line of sight blurred. Deeper, deeper, deeper...until Grant's hand pushed against her body and Faith's breathing became labored.

"Oh...fuck..." she barely whispered, her eyes rolling back. "Feels...*soooooo gooooooood...*"

The pressure eased as Grant pulled back.

Faith grasped his wrist and fell a little off-balance. "No," she begged, meeting his eyes. She pressed her forehead to his. "Please don't stop. Please don't. I've never felt anything so good."

Instead of pulling the rest of the way out, Grant thrust home.

"Ah..." Her body tightened and flooded with a kind of ecstasy she'd never experienced. She cried out and dropped her head back, body quivering.

Grant pressed a kiss to her throat, then murmured at her ear, "Let go of my hand and grip the edge of the table."

She obeyed.

"Next time you touch me without permission," he rasped, "I'm pulling out and taking all this pleasure with me."

No, no, no. She closed her eyes and swallowed, preparing herself to be patient.

But Grant started moving again. Moving inside her. Deep, deep inside her. Strokes, shallow thrusts, and pressure. Lots of pressure. The kind of pressure that made her want to move and beg. The kind that made her insane.

"I want...to come..." The words fell from her mouth.

"You're so impatient. We're going to have to work on that." He pulled from her body, and she felt so empty. But then he was back, pushing in with what felt like two fingers, bringing more pressure.

"Fuck, yes. Oh God..." He did something that made her burn and ache and crave.

"You like that?" he murmured, thrusting deep and slow with thicker penetration.

"Yes, yes, yes." She moaned and cried out and whimpered her pleasure. "Yes, yes, so good."

"You're tight, baby." He pushed, then circled, stretching her body until she burned while rubbing places that made her want to scream. "You're gonna clamp down on me like a vise, I'll lose it on my first plunge." Another moment of excruciating torture, and he murmured, "Okay, baby, give me some juice."

He stepped back, bent, and pressed his mouth to her silk-covered clit. The shock of it vanished when the warmth of his mouth overwhelmed her sex. She released the table to grab his head, but realized what she was doing and slapped her hand down on the wood again.

Grant pulled back enough to stroke the throbbing, silk-trapped flesh with his tongue. Back and forth. Back and forth. She cried out and bowed. The touch was whisper soft and warm, shocking her body with shards of intense pleasure and flooding her sex with languid heat. While inside her, he continued to do something that created a delicious pressure that kept rising and growing and intensifying. The way he watched her moan and writhe, knowing she was helpless to do anything but absorb his assault, taking what he gave, the way he gave it, added a dark, edgy intensity to the thrill, and nearly drove Faith out of her skin.

"Please, please, please..." She panted, openly begging. "Oh God...please Grant..."

Instead of licking her clit, he dragged his teeth over the silk. Bursts of electric pleasure stabbed her sex and made her whole body jerk. Then he came back with slow, smooth, warm pressure from his tongue, and Faith bowed backward, dropping her head, letting her mouth fall open on a moan. Grant rewarded her with a long moan that vibrated over her sex.

He repeated the scrape. The lick. The moan.

Faith's fingers were numb on the table's edge.

Scrape.

Lick.

Moan.

"*Fuck...*" Her entire body trembled with the need for climax.

Scrape.

Lick.

Growl.

"Grant—" She opened her eyes, lowered her head, and found his eyes on her.

She watched his mouth move over her in the scrape.

She flinched, trembled...

His tongue stroked her, slowly. But this time, with his eyes locked on hers, he continued to lave her in a lazy, hot back and forth. And he pushed deeper with his fingers. Did something that created more pressure.

A sound of surprise ebbed from her throat as she rose to the edge. Grant used his free hand to spread her sex and took her silk-covered clit between his lips, sucking and licking. Sucking and licking.

All the pressure and heat coalesced, and the orgasm roared forward, breaking in a full-body explosion. Every muscle contracted, bowing her back, twisting her waist, contorting her arms. Flash after flash after flash of ecstasy blasted through her body finally releasing her only long enough to draw air before another wave of blissfully decadent tremors racked her body.

# 9

Grant drank in the wild sight of Faith's beautiful body twisting and convulsing with pleasure. He always took satisfaction in a job well done. But this... There was something different about this. Something fierce. Something intense. He didn't know what, exactly. He just knew he'd never taken any woman's pleasure as seriously as he took Faith's. He'd always been aggressive on the ice and assertive with women, but in the bedroom, he lay back, let the woman do her thing and find her pleasure.

He had no idea where this sudden need to possess her had come from. But it burned so hot, Grant felt like it was eating a hole in his gut. A hole that could only be filled by filling her.

When she listed back against the wall, limp and panting, Grant kissed a path down the inside of her thigh, to her knee. He sat back on his heels, pulled out his wallet, and dragged out a condom.

All he could think about was pushing into all that wet heat. Driving long and hard into a pussy so tight, it would take everything Grant had to last until she came again. Later, he'd fuck her until she'd had more orgasms in one night with him than in her whole relationship with Dillon. Later he'd show her the array of orgasms awaiting her until she was so wrung out, she begged for mercy. And before the sun rose, he'd be introducing her to some rougher, edgier play sure to fire her up for the rest of his time in town.

With the condom in place, his jeans clinging to his hips, Grant dragged her panties over her hips and down her legs. He left them on the floor with the rest of her clothes and dragged her upright by her arms.

She wrapped her arms around his neck and melted into him with a long, deep, wet kiss that flashed fire back into his veins. Her mouth was loose and soft, her tongue searching and hungry. Her hands threaded in his hair and her head tilted to take the kiss deeper while her legs wrapped around him and pulled him in.

Grant stroked her body, memorizing the curves while heat and pressure continued to build at the base of his spine. He trailed his hands down her sides, over her hips, clasped her thighs, and lifted her from the table. With one turn, he pressed her back up against the wall and rocked his erection against her pussy.

She moaned into his mouth and pushed a hand between them, circling and stroking his cock. Sensation ripped a path through his pelvis and up his spine. He broke the kiss on a curse and covered her hand with his.

"You want this?" he asked.

She licked her lips. "So bad."

He moved her hand from the tip farther down the length where his girth took a significant turn, and watched her eyes widened. "You want it all? Because it's all or nothing, Faith."

"I want it all," she said without hesitation.

The girl was ballsy. He released her hand and gripped her chin. Anticipation made Grant's mouth water. "Then take it. And look me in the eye while I fill you with every fucking inch."

Lust sparked in her eyes, and her lids lowered another fraction. She was the most unique combination of sweetness and seductress. She liked the dirty talk. Liked the rough stuff. Let him have control, then played by his rules. She took her share of discomfort to get to the reward of extreme pleasure.

She was very close to winning Grant's complete respect.

But those thoughts vanished as Faith rubbed the head of his cock across her pussy, settling him at her entrance. She pressed her hand to his abdomen and licked her lips again. Grant didn't waste a second; he rocked his hips and pushed his head into her heat.

She inhaled sharply, and her eyes glazed over. Another wave of pleasure flooded Grant's body, and he gritted his teeth around a groan. But that didn't control the need to move. And after controlling himself so completely while delivering pleasure to Faith, he let go now, withdrew, and thrust again, still just a couple of inches.

"Oh *fuck*..." he rasped. She was so goddamned tight. And hot. And slick. And soft.

She was fucking heaven. And he was so fucking high on her.

"More," she murmured. "Feels so good." Her hand clutched at his gut, her nails scoring his skin. "More, more, more."

Her little pleas in that cloud-nine voice was as effective as her pussy around his cock at making him give her exactly what she wanted. He tightened his hand on her face as if that would give him a deeper connection and held her gaze as he thrust.

"Ah..."

Her little high-pitched sound of pleasure and surprise spurred him, and he rocked back, contracted the glutes he worked on all year and thrust again.

"Oh God..." She tipped back her head, pulling from his grasp, and hit the wall. "Again, again, again."

"Look...at me," he ordered in a voice that sounded like something from *The Lord of the Rings*.

She lowered her gaze, but her head listed sideways and ended up resting in his palm. And that was where she stayed as he thrust until he'd scored a path for his entire cock into her pussy and his balls slapped her flesh.

Then, leaving her shoulders against the wall, he took a step back, putting her body at a forty-five-degree angle to his. Her breath came fast and shallow. Her skin was smooth and flushed. Her body toned and supple. God, she was gorgeous. And all his.

*All his.*

His gut fluttered. He didn't understand the thrill of that. Or the drive to exploit it. But he'd have to think about that later, because his body was out of patience.

He pushed Faith's head upright and closed his fingers in her hair until she winced. "Are you ready to scream, Faith?"

Already panting, Faith licked the seam of her lips. And nodded.

Grant pulled out, engaged his glutes, and thrust. And his first free, rabid drive into Faith Nicholas was more glorious than his best fantasy. Smooth. Soft. Warm. Slick. And so fucking tight. Heaven. Absolute heaven.

Faith's hips hit the wall. The head of Grant's cock slammed Faith. And she cried out, half shock, half pleasure.

His second drive was euphoric, ending in another cry of pleasure from Faith along with a tight squeeze of her pussy.

Grant put all of himself into his work, his mission, and this moment. Faith on display and at his mercy. Her perky tits rocking, her abdominal muscles flexing, his cock impaling her sweet pussy. Their bodies in perfect sync, striving for the same goal—mutual ultimate pleasure.

"Ah God, Grant—" Her fingernails dug into his forearms,

and the sting added an edgy excitement. "Grant, fuck... So good."

Sweat slipped down his temple. It felt amazing. This was great sex. The kind that worked up a sweat when you didn't notice because it was so good, it hadn't seemed like work at all.

Faith lifted to meet him, and Grant put more power behind his thrust until his balls stung with each hit. And *fuck* that was good. Everything about this was good.

He gritted his teeth and growled, picking up speed to satisfy Faith's demands, which drove his own. Faster than he preferred. Damn woman. She fucked up his control.

"Oh my God... Oh my God..." She half laughed, half cried the words, arching, head dropped back, every muscle in her beautiful body stretched tight. A sight Grant wished he could memorize. "Ah, fuck, Gra—"

Her whole body convulsed. Her pussy cranked down on Grant's cock so hard, his throat closed. His body broke, and his orgasm slammed through him like a lightning crack. He lost his balance and put out a hand to catch the wall, wrapping his other arm around Faith, and steadied them as they both floated back to baseline.

Once Grant's muscles released the last orgasmic quake, they gave. Still, he reluctantly pulled from Faith's body, making a mental note to take her to bed next time so they could both sink into a comfortable mattress after. Then set her down. She wasn't any more stable, using the wall to keep herself up.

He wrapped the condom in a tissue from a box he'd pushed to the floor earlier and tossed it in the trash, then looked around at the mess he'd made. He scratched his head. "I'll... clean this up in the morning."

"Holy. Shit." Her whisper drew Grant's gaze back. She was scraping a hand through her hair and pulling it off her face. A face flushed and relaxed, with a look of awe and shock in her eyes.

He slipped his arm around her waist, pulled her close, and kissed her neck. She pressed her cheek to his chest and ran her nails lightly up his side, sending tingles over his skin.

Warmth and affection swamped Grant out of nowhere. "I can't remember the last time it's been that good."

She lifted her heavy-lidded gaze to his. "So it's not just me?"

He smiled. "Oh, it's you baby." He kissed her. Softly. Slowly. And sighed. "It's definitely you."

# 10

"Baby," Grant called from the ground, "this is a fantastic view of your perfect ass, but I gotta tell you, you're freaking me out."

She laughed and dropped her hand from the roof's eave to press a hand to her stomach, aching from all the laughing she'd done with him today. And all the sexual gymnastics he'd put her through the night before. "Would you stop? I'm almost finished, and it's getting dark."

"You're not almost finished," he complained. "You still have the whole front, which includes three more gables. But you're right about it getting dark. I swear my heart's not going to make it through this. If you hurt yourself, you won't be able to set up for the Winter—whatchamacallit."

"Winter Wonderland," she corrected him for the third time.

"I don't care. Get your beautiful self down here. I'll finish the rest."

Grinning, she hooked the end of the light string to the corner of the gable, then twisted to look down at him. He was standing at the base of the ladder, holding it stable with one gloved hand, aiming the video camera at her with the other. He looked adorable all bundled up in his parka, a knit hat warming his head, his dark hair sneaking out from underneath the edges, and a few days of scruff darkening his jaw.

"You may have gotten away with telling me what to do last night," she said, "but don't expect that to continue during the day."

He lowered the camera with a big, bright grin cutting across his face. "Is that right?"

"Yeah, that's right. And you'd better be able to dub over that tape like you promised or all this effort is going to be wasted."

"Someone's getting bossy," he told her as she climbed down the ladder. "Sounds like she needs a spanking."

As soon as she got within his reach, Grant slapped her ass. Hard.

Faith gasped. "Ow." She half laughed the complaint and shot a scowl over her shoulder. "You little—"

Another crack stung her cheek. Her sex clenched and flooded with heat, shocking her.

"No name-calling," he told her.

Faith gritted her teeth against the flare of desire. This had been happening all day—these sudden, intense bursts of lust, erupting out of nowhere like the strike of a match. She'd chalked it up to residual hunger from their wicked night, a desire awoken from hibernation and greedy for fuel. And after a day of close proximity and teasing, she was seriously ready to do something reckless for a fix.

She continued down the ladder, stopping a couple of rungs from the bottom to turn to face him, eye to eye. He circled her in his arms and stepped close until their jacket-clad bodies pressed. She wrapped her arms around his neck and stroked her hand across his rough cheek. "I may be laying down a few of my own rules tonight, Saber. So don't get too comfortable with all this *control*."

"Mmm." He set the camera on a higher rung and squeezed her butt, pulling her closer. "I like the sound of that."

And he kissed her.

The move had become familiar over the course of the day. He'd hatched this filming plan the night before during lulls in their sexual activity. And later today, after the store had closed and he finished with the high school hockey practice, he'd promised to show her how to take the video from camera to YouTube.

Before Faith had even stirred from their nonstop night of bliss, Grant had repaired the broken pipe in her basement, then driven into Ashville, the next largest city, to buy a video camera and video editing software. And he'd followed her with that damn camera all afternoon, recording nonstop.

He'd also been touching her nonstop, kissing her nonstop, and smiling nonstop. Her passion had built and built, filling her with an ache she wanted him to ease. And the way he was adding to that fire with his teasing, talented tongue wasn't helping her ignore her desire.

Faith slowly, reluctantly pulled from the kiss and stroked his jaw, running her thumb over his bottom lip. "Have I mentioned you're the best kisser in the entire universe?"

Grinning, he pressed his lips to her forehead. "Maybe, but I doubt anyone could hear that enough."

His lips trailed over her cheek and down her neck. Faith hummed in pleasure. "Have I mentioned last night was the best night of my life, and that I can't wait to get you naked again?"

"Maybe," he murmured against her throat, gripping her ass with both hands and pulling her hips against his, making her groan. "But tell me again." He lifted his head, brushed her hair off her forehead, and cradled her jaw. "Tell me in a way you haven't told me before."

She sighed. Her gut ached. Her body yearned. Faith met his

eyes. "Last night...opened a new chapter in my life. You make me feel...strong and treasured and beautiful in a way I've never felt before. You make me realize there's more to life than Holly and St. Nicholas Hardware. I was starting to believe I wasn't capable of handling things on my own. You changed that."

His devilish smile had softened into a look of surprise. He didn't say anything for a long moment, just searched her eyes. "Really?"

"Really."

"I...don't know what to say. No one's ever..."

She shook her head and kissed him lightly. "Don't say anything. You asked, I answered. Now let me go so I can move the ladder. The sooner I get this done, the sooner I can get you back to bed. And I'm *dying* to get you back to bed."

She stepped to the ground and turned toward the ladder. Gripping the sides, she pulled it carefully away from the house.

Grant's hands covered hers and pushed the ladder back against the house with a clatter.

"Grant..." she said, annoyed.

She cut a look over her shoulder just as one of his arms circled her waist and hauled her up against him, forcing all the air from her lungs. But there was no mistaking the erection pressed against the curve of her ass. Or the rasp of desire in his voice when he put his lips to her temple and said, "Why wait?"

Faith fought to pull her gray matter back together. "Why wait for what?"

"To take the edge off that need."

She groaned and rubbed against him. "Because you have practice in half an hour, I have to close the store, and there are lights hanging off Dwayne's roof. If you'd stop distracting me, I'd get it done."

"If you let me do it, it would get done faster."

"Says you."

"I don't want you up on that ladder in the dark."

"Same. And you need to let your shoulder rest. You're supposed to be *recuperating*, remember?"

"I stopped by another store while I was in Ashville." One of his hands moved lower, pressed between her legs, and closed over her sex.

Shock and excitement twined. She sucked a breath and rocked away from his hand, only to meet with more pressure behind her from his hips…and that iron swell. "Grant, Dwayne's going to be home soon." She glanced around the front yard, to the quiet street and the houses with lights shining in the windows surrounding them. "And we're *in public*."

"Don't you want to know which store?"

He gripped her sex tighter and all the built-up lust from the last twenty-four hours spilled between her legs. A groan ebbed from Faith's throat.

"Naughty," he whispered with wicked glee at her ear. "Bet you didn't even know it was there. I swear it was like a speakeasy, the front door off an alley and unmarked."

He clenched and released her sex as he spoke, and within thirty seconds, Faith was dizzy with the same clawing need he'd instilled in her the night before.

Without warning, his hand disappeared from between her legs, and while a minute ago all she'd been able to think about was getting him to stop, now all she could think about was getting his touch back.

The man seriously messed with her mind.

"I want to show you one of the little treats I picked up for you."

While he reached into his pocket, Faith forced her head clear. She pushed at his arm wrapped around her waist, but he held her in a vise. And the more she moved, the more she rubbed his erection, exciting them both.

"I want to see it," she told him, "*after* I'm done with the lights."

"I can't wait that long." He reached around her with the other hand and jerked at the button on her jeans, making her gasp. "And I don't think you can either."

"Grant, what in the hell—"

His bare hand pushed against her belly and slid down, down, down. Beneath her panties and deep between her legs. The warmth and pressure combined to swamp Faith with pleasure and lust and a need so rabid, it clawed at her.

She grabbed a rung of the ladder with one hand and curled the fingers of the other around Grant's wrist. But that didn't keep her from rocking against his hand as if she had no control over her body. "Ah...my *God*."

"That's just the beginning," he rasped at her ear. He did something with his fingers, kicking off a vibration.

"Wh—what—"

He opened his mouth on her neck and pushed his hand deep with a low groan. Something attached to one or two of his fingers vibrated over her sex.

"H-holy—" A wicked and wild pleasure cut off any ability to think. "Oh my *God*."

"You can't wait, can you?" he asked.

She couldn't answer. The only thing she could focus on was the buzz between her legs making her go cross-eyed.

He stroked circles around and around her opening. Faith's mouth dropped open, and her breathing grew choppy. *Holy fuck. Holy fuck. Holy fuck.* She would have said the words if she'd been able to speak. This level of pleasure was unthinkable until this moment. And just when she thought it couldn't get any better, just when she saw the horizon of that delicious orgasm she'd been craving for hours, Grant pushed two fingers past her opening and up into her pussy.

Two thick, vibrating fingers.

She cried out in pleasure, in shock, in need.

"Shh, shh..." Grant's whisper at her ear dragged her back down to earth. "We're in public, remember?"

Holy shit. She forced her eyes to focus. The night had grown a little darker, but not dark enough for Faith to be letting him do what he was doing. Nor did she have *any* intention of stopping him. And just how twisted was that?

"Need more room." The hand at her waist pushed her zipper down and wiggled her jeans lower on her hips. Then he stroked over her ass, down her thigh, and caught her behind the knee. And lifted her foot to the second ladder rung. "There we go..."

The fingers inside her moved freely, pushing deep, immediately finding the place that made her moan and whimper and bend and shatter, and manipulating it mercilessly with those soft, vibrating fingertips.

The sensation gushing through her pulled Faith into an arch with a high-pitched "Oh God..." Her head dropped back against Grant's shoulder, mouth open with sounds she absolutely could not control. "Yes, yes, yes."

God, she'd used that word a lot over the last twenty-four hours. *Yes* and *more* and *please*. More than she'd used them in all her years combined.

Grant covered her hand curled around his wrist and pried her fingers loose. "I need more room, baby."

With his hand over hers, he pushed them both beneath the hem of her tee, up her abdomen, and beneath one bra cup, so her own hand covered her breast. She barely noticed when his other hand pushed even deeper inside her and Grant finger-fucked her in long, slow, deep, vibrating strokes.

He thrust deep, rubbing her back wall with the vibration and rasping, "You are so fucking sexy." Then twisted his hand and pulled out halfway, holding it there to circle and circle and circle. "I can't wait to get you naked and use this all over your body."

"Don't stop, don't stop," she begged.

"Touch yourself, Faith," he whispered at her ear. "Pinch and roll your nipple."

She did, without question, without resistance. He'd broken down barrier after sexual barrier in one twenty-four-hour period and conditioned her for pleasure. And his murmured "Good girl" tipped her closer to the edge.

"Oh, fuck, please, Grant. Harder, harder, harder."

"Mmmm, damn, baby, you're a trip."

He thrust deep and hard, and pleasure exploded through her body. "Yes, yes, yes. More, more, more."

"Talk dirty to me, Faith."

Always pushing her. This was how he did it. He got her to this place where she needed release, craved the pleasure, then pushed her for one more inch.

"Give it to me," she said, her voice thin and rough. "If you're going to fuck me, fuck me, don't play with me."

His laugh was quick and hot, followed by a growl of fire and deep, steady, hard thrusts of vibration.

"Ah, God... Don't stop. Don't fucking stop. So good. Mmm, so good. Can't wait, can't—"

She shattered with a scream of shock and ecstasy—one Grant cut off with his hand over her mouth. One he perpetuated with continued hard thrusts and manipulation of her G-spot. Faith could have been in the middle of a crowd and not given a damn at that moment. All that mattered was soaking up every last drop of bliss spilling through her body.

Faith was panting and still shaking when her mind came to a sluggish focus. She leaned against him, while Grant's hand stayed between her legs and continued to explore her. "I *love* how wet you get."

"What...in the hell...is that?" she asked, barely able to keep her eyes open. Her skin tingled everywhere he touched, and he was getting adventurous.

"A fucking fantastic investment is what this is. That store in Ashville was the best find ever." His fingers stroked her perineum, and her blood kicked right back to simmer. She rocked her hips back against him, and he groaned. "Imagine having me inside you, filling you, stretching you, hammering you, while I run these over your body."

That thought pushed her breath right out of her lungs. "How long until Dwayne gets back?"

He chuckled, low and hot. Leaning over her, he kissed her throat, grazed the skin with his teeth, and pushed his fingers farther back, vibrating a path between her cheeks.

A zing of sexual current cut through her ass, and she gasped. He worked circles over the pucker there and shot Faith right back toward climax. "Oh *fuck*... Grant..."

Her whine was wasted on him. His mouth bit paths along her neck while his vibrating fingers stimulated a whole new and intense response. And he dragged her hand, still beneath his own, into her pants and placed her fingers over her clit.

"Touch," he said.

"Grant—"

"*Touch*." His order was final, and he maneuvered her fingers to the very top of her clit, where his fingers joined hers in searching for that place—

He found it first, and his touch pushed more pleasure into Faith's sex from a whole different direction. She was bombarded with sensations so wildly thrilling, she wanted to drown in them. Swim in them. She whimpered but let Grant place his fingers with hers. Let him guide her movement.

He lowered his chin, putting his lips at her ear. "Do you have *any* idea how *fucking hot* it makes me to *watch you* touch yourself?"

A whole different kind of pleasure filled Faith. She pried

her eyes open and found his handsome face in the darkening shadows, creased with desire and intensity.

"Now you can find pleasure and satisfaction any time you want it, Faith. No more denying yourself."

Emotion rolled through her, intense and sharp. Emotion she didn't understand. She released the ladder and curved her arm back and around Grant's head, pulling his mouth to hers. And gifted him with an erotic example of what she hoped he'd do to her when they had more privacy.

He drank her in, added passion to the kiss, and devoured her while his fingers parted, pushed Faith's out of the way and shocked her clit with an orgasm that burned right to her core. Grant added pressure to her mouth to keep her from pulling away and muffled her cries as he drove orgasm after sweet orgasm through her body until she dropped back against him, limp.

Grant still had his hand down her pants when headlights turned the corner and started down the street.

"You, Miss Nicholas, have been saved by the cavalry." He dragged his hand back and jerked her jacket into place a moment before Dwayne turned into his drive. And pushed the vibrating fingertips into his jacket pocket. "Because I was just about ready to do you in the front yard. Damn, you make me do the craziest thing, woman."

Grant was teasing, but in her exhausted state, it struck her as extremely funny. She was holding herself up with the ladder, still laughing, when Dwayne climbed from his car, grinning.

"What are you two up to?" he wanted to know.

"Faith just lost at rock paper scissors," Grant told him, taking Faith by the arm and sitting her on the front steps. "Now she's got to sit on her ass while I finish the gables."

"Hey..." she complained, then started laughing again. "That's only because you wouldn't let me go for three out of five." And she added a sweet "The offer's still open."

That made Grant bust up laughing. “I promise to take you up on that another time. But not right this minute.” He grabbed the ladder and walked it to the next gable, telling Dwayne, “We’ll be ready for a show in ten minutes. Get your popcorn ready.”

# 11

"Okay, here we go, boys," Grant called once the kids were in position for their last drill of the night. "Remember, you're passing while you're moving, so make sure to whip that puck hard to get it in front of your teammate. Then pivot, catch the shot from the next man down the line, and shoot it up the ice."

He blew his whistle, and the kids glided into action. Grant floated on the edge of the rink and rolled his shoulder while his gaze focused on the kids' feet and hands, on pivots and shots.

Dwayne paced the sidelines. "Stay low in your turns, boys. Keep movin', keep movin', shoot."

"Talk it up, guys," Grant told them. "You should always be talkin' to each other out there. If you want something, call for it. Pick up the pace, boys. Giddyap, let's go."

"Giddyap?" Dwayne said, shooting him an incredulous grin. "Is that the shit they teach you in the big leagues?"

"Shut up." Grant grinned. "Parker, *move* those feet. Whoa, Healy, what the hell was that? You control the puck, the puck doesn't control you."

That brought some laughter. "Good," he called out encouragement. "Nice." And as the last few members of the team passed up the ice, Grant clapped to get the team's attention. "Other way, same drill. Speed, accuracy, focus. *Go*."

His phone chimed. Without looking away from the boys, he answered, but instead of saying hello, he lowered the mouthpiece and yelled, "Jordy, you here to socialize or practice? Cut the bullshit. If I have to tell you again, the whole team's gonna be doing sprints."

A collective groan rolled through the group, and Jordy received a number of shoulder shoves, which shut him right up.

Smiling, Grant lifted the phone to his mouth. "Grant."

"Hey." A male voice that he didn't immediately recognize sounded over the line. "Sounds like you're as much of a hard-ass with teenagers as you are with grown men."

By the time he finished speaking, Grant recognized his younger brother's voice. "Do you mean on the ice or with you? 'Cause I haven't seen you enough to be a hard-ass yet."

"I know," Patrick said, "that's why I'm here to take you for a beer when you're done."

Grant heard stereo and turned to find his Patrick strolling toward the rink, one hand in his pocket, huddled in a parka. Patrick grinned and lowered his phone. Grant had mixed feelings about his brother's appearance. On the one hand, he was the reason their parents had even entertained the idea of seeing one of Grant's games. On the other, Grant really wanted to go straight back to the store, pack in some quality Faith time—preferably buried deep inside her, driving her to scream his name the way she had last night, then teaching her how to edit video and set up her YouTube account. And, yeah, then work on more screaming.

Damn, his cock was already half-hard just thinking about it.

"Patrick?" Dwayne turned and held his hand out to Grant's brother, but he didn't look all that happy to see him. Still,

Patrick stepped up and shook Dwayne's hand. "Haven't seen you in a while."

"Yeah." He released Dwayne's hand and scraped it through his hair, looking at the ground. "Well, I'm sure no one missed me." He looked up and met Dwayne's eyes. "But I'm clean and sober, eight months now."

Shock hit Grant in the stomach. He'd known Patrick had a problem, but not that it had been acknowledged or that he'd sought help or that he'd been successful at battling the addiction.

"Congratulations, kid."

Patrick grinned. "Thanks, thanks."

"Grant, you go on," Dwayne said. "I've got this. I'll see you tomorrow."

Grant nodded. "Thanks."

He sat down, threw on his blade guards and started unlacing his skates.

"Thank you," Dwayne said. "And tell Faith thank you again too. I've been getting all sorts of calls and texts about the lights. You made a lot of people happy tonight."

Dwayne skated toward the kids calling directions while Grant pushed into tennis shoes.

"What lights?" Patrick asked.

"The ones on his house. The system's been down since MaryAnn passed, and we helped him get it up and running again."

He set his skates in his duffel, tossed it over his shoulder, and started toward the parking lot with Patrick, but his mind was on how happy Faith would be to hear how the lights were affecting the community.

His brother wrapped a playful arm around Grant's neck and wrestled him, singing, "Someone's got a crush..."

Grant laughed and pushed Patrick off. "You're still not big enough to do that."

Patrick straightened, making a face at how he topped Grant's height by two inches.

"*Old enough*," Grant corrected. "You'll always be my *baby* brother."

"Who's Faith?"

"Let's talk about you. Why did you invite me for a beer if you're sober?"

"Because it's the socially polite thing to do. And because it's good practice. And because I always feel a little stronger when I walk out of a bar still able to count backward from one hundred. Who's Faith?"

Grant ignored his last Faith inquiry and focused on the glimmer of the good-natured kid his brother had once been. That made Grant smile.

They agreed to take separate cars and meet at Yuletide Spirits. Grant planned on walking from there to Faith's and staying with her tonight, and he didn't want anything interfering with that plan.

As he pulled out of the parking lot, he dialed Faith.

"Hey, handsome," she answered. "Hope you didn't send any of the kids home with marks."

"Not a one."

"Good boy."

And here came their first test. "So...my brother found me at the rink. We're going to grab a beer."

"Really?" She sounded surprised, but in a good way. Grant held his hopes back, waiting for the other shoe to drop. "Which one?"

"Patrick."

"That's great."

He was still waiting. "Why is that great? You don't like my brothers."

"I don't like how your brothers *act*. I don't know your brothers as people, so I couldn't tell you whether I like them or not. And it's great because I have no doubt you'll be a positive influence for him. Have fun."

He frowned, a little unsure what to do without conflict to deal with. "What are you doing?"

"Well," she said, sounding far too chipper for a woman who'd been up all night, worked all day, and been dealt two ginormous orgasms a couple of hours ago. "I finished making notes on the instructions I want to record over the video, and I just started putting supplies together for the festival. My back room looks like Parties Unlimited USA."

He smiled. "I'll help when I get there."

"I've got it. You don't get to see your family much, and you don't have much time left in town. Enjoy yourself." A familiar bell rang in the background. "I've got to run to the front. I'll talk to you later, okay?"

"Yeah. Sure. Bye."

"Bye."

Grant stopped at a red light behind his brother's Mercedes SUV and frowned at his phone where it rested on his thigh. "Have fun?"

Where was the self-invitation to join them? The pissy attitude over him going out without her? The pouting?

"Enjoy myself?"

The light turned green, and he continued toward town. Halfway there, he caught himself trying to twist her words into something negative. And laughed at himself, relieved he was making it up. "God, I'm an idiot."

But that relief didn't last long, because then he was thinking about her *"You don't have much time left in town."*

He really didn't. The team was off for the holidays now, but they'd head back to practice in less than a week. Then they'd dive into a grueling schedule of games, practices, and special events, packed into nearly every day straight through the middle of June.

And Grant would be with them.

He couldn't wait. Couldn't wait to be with his guys. Back on a schedule. Battling for every play on the ice.

But it also meant he had to leave Faith. His first thought was to ask her if she'd continue seeing him, but Grant didn't have to look at a schedule to know there would only be one short break over the next six months when he'd be able to fly here and see her. Nor did he have to fathom a guess of how often she'd be free to come see him. Not with a struggling store, limited funds, and that damn iron pride of hers. He had no doubt they'd end up in a fight if he even brought up the subject of paying for her travel. Beyond that, she hadn't shown any serious interest in hockey. She listened to him talk about his career and his buddies, but when he started talking strategy, her eyes glazed over.

Not that it mattered… Did it?

"Why in the hell am I even thinking these things?" he asked the empty car.

After a moment, his mind answered: because he knew that by June, when he could come spend the summer with her, she'd be gone. If not physically gone because she'd sold the store, she'd be taken by some young stud who knew a good thing when he saw it.

Grant's mood plummeted. The discomfort only added to his stress. He shouldn't be this affected by a woman he'd known for a week and a half. That was insane.

He pulled into a spot in front of Faith's store, while his brother pulled in a block away at the bar. Grant cut the engine and the lights and stared inside at the light glowing in the back. He wanted to bail on Patrick and go help Faith. He wanted to *be* with Faith.

He hadn't realized how long he'd been sitting there until Patrick strolled up to his door.

"Dude." His voice sounded muffled through the glass. "Are

you drunk already? The bar is over there. This is—" A look came over Patrick's face. He darted a glance at the hardware store, then looked back at Grant. "Ooooh, wait." He pointed to the store. "Is *this* the Faith you're crushing on?"

"*Shut up.*" Grant climbed from the car, annoyed. "Just tell the whole town."

Patrick chuckled and turned in a slow circle. "Bro, look around you."

True, there wasn't a damn soul on the frozen street. And, yes, that just irritated Grant more.

"Huh," Patrick said, an amused look of confusion crossing his face. "I didn't see that one coming."

Grant wondered what Patrick saw that he didn't. "Why not?"

He shrugged. "You've always gone for the hoity-toity type."

"How do you know who I date?"

Now Patrick lifted his brows. "Hel-lo. Have you not heard of this newfangled thing called the Internet? Have you also not noticed that you are one of the top fifty best-paid NHL players in the nation? I keep telling everyone I'm not as dumb as I look. Nobody listens. Anyway, I'm sure you're already aware of this, but you may want to know for future reference that every time you date someone, the press wants to sneak into your bedroom and take pictures. So, yeah, I know you go for the high-maintenance chicks. Faith's real pretty. She's just kinda...I don't know, simple, in comparison. But then we are in Holly, North Carolina, not Washington, DC. What's a guy gonna do?"

While Grant was surprised and, yeah, even pleased, that his brother had developed enough interest in Grant's career to actually look him up, there was also enough truth to Patrick's statement to turn Grant downright surly. But he couldn't blame anyone for that except himself.

Still, he shoved Patrick's shoulder in the direction of the bar. "Do you want me to buy you a tonic and lime or not?"

"Ho, look at you, big spender. But I actually prefer root beer nowadays. Think you could manage a root beer?"

Grant laughed.

"And maybe some pretzels?" Patrick asked.

"Okay, now you're pushing it."

Patrick thought that was hilarious and laughed his way toward Yuletide Spirits.

Grant followed, grinning reluctantly. His brother had come back from the brink of disaster and not just survived but thrived. It seemed like he might even have become fun again.

"And, for the record," Patrick said as they came up to the bar's front door, "I'm all for you looking at changing the type of women you see." He paused at the steps and turned to Grant. "My girlfriend and I have been together six months. She's nothing like the women I usually drifted toward, but she's at least half the reason I was successful at rehab, about twenty percent of the reason I'm still sober, and accounts for ninety-five percent of my happiness. She's the best fuckin' thing that ever happened to me."

Grant grinned. "Hey, man. That's great."

Patrick nodded and continued up the stairs to the doors. "Faith's always been a real nice girl. Even when I wasn't so nice to her, she believed I could be and do better. She's worth taking a long, hard look at, bro."

His brother pushed into the bar, but Grant stood there a moment, absorbing the wisdom his little brother had just bestowed upon him. Grant already knew Faith was beautiful—inside and out. But his brother's experience of internal transformation with the love of the right woman, spoke to something Grant had been trying to pin down for the last couple of days.

When Grant got a minute to himself, he was going to have to start thinking about his own life and how he might manage to pull his head out of his ass.

# 12

Faith piled one more extension cord on the mountain of supplies needed for the ice-sculpting competition and checked that box off her list. "Done."

She leaned against the wall, hung her head, and closed her eyes. God, she was so tired. And not just no-sleep tired, but her-body-hurt-in-a-million-new-ways tired. Ways that made her smile, despite the discomfort.

The thought of Grant hanging with his brother warmed her heart, and she couldn't wait to hear about their talk after years of estrangement. She didn't like Patrick as a drunk or a womanizer or a compulsive liar-borderline-narcissist. But she'd heard he'd been sober for a while and hoped his time with Grant gave them both a little healing from the wounds their family carried.

At the same time, it made her sad. She missed her dad. Last night, falling asleep in Grant's arms, was the first night she hadn't cried herself to sleep in longer than she could remember. Faith knew it wouldn't be the end to the loneliness or the tears, but she was deeply grateful for the reprieve and the glimmer of hope he'd given her.

And, yeah, she realized there would be another gaping hole

in her life when he went back to DC after Christmas. But she'd deal with it when it happened. She certainly wasn't going to rush it one second faster than she had to. Faith was going to enjoy that boy right down to the wire, and when it was time to let him go, she'd let him go. And she'd be happy for him, because he'd be going back where he belonged, with people who loved and respected him. Who understood and supported him.

She couldn't want more than that.

Except...

Her mind whirled with possibilities that were really just pure fantasy. Faith laughed at herself and shook the impossible from her mind so she didn't get unnecessarily hurt when this little fling ended.

She rubbed at tired eyes and refocused on the list. The door to her store chimed, and Faith pulled her phone from her back pocket to check the time. But even before she could begin to wonder who would stop in at this late hour, the light clip-clip-clip of high heels sounded in the store.

Dread coiled in the pit of her stomach. She rolled her eyes to the ceiling and told her dad, "Leaving me to deal with her was cruel and unusual punishment."

"Faith?" Natalie called. "Where are you?"

"Back here." She set the list aside and straightened the supplies headed to the festival tomorrow.

Natalie came around the corner, and her pretty blue eyes immediately skated over the mound of supplies. "Oh, is that all for our artists?"

Faith smiled. The Art League liked to think everyone involved with their organization was an "artist," but Faith knew for a fact there were a lot of rednecks who brought their chainsaws and twelve-packs out to this event in the hope of winning a prize or two.

"It is."

"And you're on schedule for setup tomorrow?"

"I am."

"You do know of the large number of last-minute registrants?"

"I do. It's fantastic."

"Isn't it?" Natalie exhaled and gave Faith that plastic smile. "It's the biggest turnout for the contest in the history of the festival. Grant's really pulling in money for the community. I just want to make sure—"

"Grant?" Faith's gut tingled, but not in a good way.

"Yes, Grant. I know you've been...spending time with him. I was coming home from my sister's bridal shower late last night. And I mean late—we Duboix girls really know how to party—and I noticed his car here."

Discomfort tightened inside her. Her father had been gone only six months. She didn't want to appear to be gleefully making use of his absence by sleeping with random men. It might be irrational, but she knew how people talked, and he'd given so much to this town. They both had. She didn't want his memory tarnished in any way.

So, even though her relationship with Grant was none of Natalie's business, she said, "I had an emergency water leak in the basement. Grant was nice enough to help me fix my pipes."

Natalie gave a low, edgy laugh. "I'm sure he did. Grant's fixed the pipes of half the women on Manhattan's list of most eligible bachelorettes. But just so we're clear, he's with me for the festival. We're MCing ice-carving together, we're judging together, we're going to the awards banquet together. We've also got plans to spend the evening together afterward."

Anger flared, pushing a flash of heat through Faith's neck and face. She bypassed the whole Grant issue for the moment and went straight for the knife in her heart. "Hold on. I don't know what you're talking about. *I'm* judging."

"It's all over the fliers we sent out. They're posted in your windows, Faith. The reason we have so many entrants is because *Grant* is judging this year."

Embarrassment washed in and joined her anger. How could she have missed something so important? "I don't have time to read every line of the marketing campaigns others hang in my window. And the fact that you didn't come to me directly but waited until the posters were printed, and told me at the last minute is pure cowardice."

"Think what you like, Faith, but the fact is that things change. I'm really sorry about your daddy. But his vision for this festival has always been about turning the pockets of the people around here inside out and getting those coins flowing into the streets of Holly. Grant is a golden ticket to that end, and creating a unified front between the biggest guest sponsor and the charity's CEO is key to securing large donations from the deepest pockets. Corporate pockets."

Faith instantly connected the dots of this twisted manipulation right back to Grant's mother, Hazel.

"Now, I don't expect you to understand that with your one year of college and all," Natalie said, "but corporations look for certain marketing elements when they're considering large donations. Strong, cohesive marketing strategies in a business—or charity in this case—run by savvy executives. I'm sure you can see how showing those potential donors the dovetailed presentation of charity, sponsor, and celebrity will be the key to securing big money for Holly."

Natalie slapped on that dry, condescending smile. "And isn't that what this festival is all about? Isn't that what your daddy would have wanted?"

Livid. Faith was *livid*. In some distant part of her mind, she recognized that her anger was out of proportion to the situation. But in the scope of her life's downward spiral, her emotions were far, far stronger than her rationale.

She took one giant, menacing step toward Natalie and

reaped far too much satisfaction from the way the other woman's bright blue eyes widened.

"What you and Grant do is up to you," she told Natalie, "but my dad *started* this damn festival, and it's still running and bringing money into this community because *my dad* kept it going *every fucking year*. A *decade* before you even *existed*. So don't you *dare* act like you know more about the business of fundraising, because *he* raised money for this town to pay for *your* education." Faith stabbed Natalie's chest with one rigid finger. "And *your* summer camps"—stab—"and *your* after-school care"—stab—"because *your* parents"—stab—"were too fucking busy to raise a *decent* human being, and *my* father still cared."

When Faith stopped to draw a breath, she realized she'd pushed Natalie several feet across the sales floor toward the exit. And the other woman was looking at Faith like she'd gone insane.

She might have snapped a nerve, but she wasn't insane. She was tired of pretending everything was okay. She was tired of giving, giving, giving and not getting anything back. She was tired of not standing up for herself, for ignoring her own needs and putting others first.

Grant had taught her that. Grant had taught her a lot of things.

"You're clearly not thinking straight," Natalie said, turning toward the door. "We'll talk about this—"

Faith grabbed Natalie's arm. She collected herself and kept her voice low and level but made sure her steel tone was crystal clear. "We'll finish this right now. You're *not* taking this away from me, because I'm *not* letting go. So if you want light, power, water, tables, and chairs at that festival, Natalie, you'll step out of the judging lineup."

When the woman's mouth thinned into a stubborn line,

Faith added, "If you want a fight, you'll get one. And I promise you won't only lose, but you will *never* live it down."

Natalie jerked from Faith's grasp with a disgusted huff and stalked to the door, flinging it open. Her dramatic exit was foiled when the anti-slam hinges Faith had installed kept the door from hitting the wall. Little did Faith realize she wasn't installing them as much for the children of Holly as she was for the adults who acted worse than children.

But long after Natalie disappeared into the night, Faith was left with Natalie's words eating away at her. She turned to get back to work so she could forget that she had no say in what Grant did or who he did it with. To ignore the hurt of knowing she was no more special to him than any other woman. And to work off the anger of getting extra mad at herself for placing her self-worth on a man's view of her.

Only, she realized, depending on Natalie's decision, she might not be delivering all these supplies to the festival. Which meant she'd just placed the success of the festival and the influx of money for Holly and all the good people here on the shoulders of an immature, self-centered, spoiled little bitch.

And that was when the repercussions of her anger registered. And her shame sank in.

Her father would be *so* disappointed in her.

Faith's heart dropped clear to her feet. She leaned back against the sales counter, covered her face with both hands, and started bawling.

# 13

Grant virtually bounced up the steps to the hardware store after his time with Patrick. His brother had developed into a remarkable businessman, and once he'd gotten Faith's story out of Grant, they'd talked in depth about the possibilities for her future. And he couldn't wait to share them with her.

But when he reached the top step, he realized the store was dark and the closed sign was up on the door. Disappointment snuck in, but when he tried the door, it opened. He stepped in and listened, but heard silence. "Faith?"

No answer. Grant looked at the door leading to her apartment but didn't start that direction. She'd probably crashed early. And after what he'd put her through last night, he really should let her get some rest.

When he turned toward the front of the store again, his gaze passed over the sales center, where a piece of paper taped to a register caught his eye.

It read:

*Grant, I'm upstairs. Please lock the front door before you come up.*

He relaxed and smiled. His body flipped from off to on. From dark to light. From depressed to exhilarated.

Oh, hell, yeah. This was definitely different.

He turned and locked the front door, then pulled the note off the register and tossed it into the trash on his way to the apartment door, but paused when he caught sight of the back room. It was packed, floor to ceiling, wall to wall with equipment. One look and Grant knew it had taken her all night to collect, haul, and stack everything into that space. He also knew she hadn't had any help. Her employees would have been taking care of the store, and Grant would bet his brand-new Rover that she'd sent them all home on time.

He looked at the door to her apartment, then dropped his gaze to his hand on the knob. But what he saw was all in his head—and it was Faith's world in the big picture. He saw who she was, where she'd been, and the mountains she still faced in her future. He saw her stresses, her fears, and all the commitments she honored out of loyalty or love.

A profound sense of humility came over him. He'd been away from his roots too long. He'd been living that fast life with no outside perspective. He'd forgotten just how hard the average American worked every day to stretch those monthly ends until they meet. That took sacrifice and dedication and perseverance. It took hard work and even a certain amount of skill. All the elements Grant had always believed set him apart and made him one of the greatest hockey players in the NHL.

But the truth was, there were a hell of a lot of people who had the same qualities. They just didn't have thousands of eyes on them nearly every night, eight months out of the year.

Like Faith.

The band around his heart, one he'd only become aware of last night, tightened just a little more, spilling fear into his body. And fear was an awkward, unfamiliar, painful emotion Grant would rather not experience. It was the reason he'd pushed his fucked-up family away. It was the reason he didn't get serious with women.

He looked up at the door again and realized... "It's too fuckin' late for that."

He was serious about wanting Faith Nicholas.

The concrete revelation took an edge off his thrill of getting upstairs with the hope of finding Faith lying naked in bed, waiting for him. But he pulled the door open and noted the silence. She was probably passed out. And that was okay. He liked the idea of just sliding into bed next to her and watching her sleep awhile. Maybe he'd take a nap himself, then wake her in the night...

That put the smile back on his face and helped his feet move up the stairs a little easier.

Halfway up, his ear caught a voice—but not Faith's. At the top of the stairs, he found the living room empty and dark and turned toward her bedroom. He stopped in the doorway and found her lying on her bed, curled on her side, with her back toward the door. Her head was propped on her hand and she was watching a video on Grant's laptop. He'd left it here that morning, along with the video editing software. She wore pale pink sink pajama bottoms that rode low on her hips and a matching tank with spaghetti straps.

Just the sight of her closed a gap in Grant's life and set everything right. He leaned his shoulder against the doorframe and exhaled, smiling.

She sniffled and glanced over her shoulder. "Oh, hey." She turned back to the screen. "I was just watching some videos to see if I could learn anything about the software you bought."

Something was wrong. Like majorly wrong. Even if Grant hadn't heard it in her voice, he could feel it in the room.

"It's pretty good." Sniffle. A clandestine wipe of her eyes. "Have you used this software before? Are they all pretty much the same? How long do you think it would take me to edit a film like the one you took today once I got the hang of it?"

He inched toward the bed, worried and—*sonofabitch*—scared. He was *scared*. He was never scared.

Beside the bed, he reached down and stroked his hand up her arm. She was warm and soft. Even from where he stood, he could smell her sweet fresh-from-the-shower scent. And man, did that stir his hunger. But Grant banked that need. "Baby, what happened?"

"Nothing." She cleared her throat. "How's your brother doing?"

"Really good." He put a knee on the bed beside her and leaned over to close the lid on his laptop.

"Hey, buddy," she tried to joke, "I was watching that."

He smiled down at her, but the first look at her face punched him in the gut, and his humor faded. Her eyes were red and swollen, still glistening with tears. The sight felt like a knife in his gut. "What's wrong?"

She rested back against his leg and offered a weak smile. "God, it's good to see you."

Christ. If he hadn't already tipped over the edge for her, this moment would have pushed him.

He ran his hand over her silky hair, and kissed her. She opened to him immediately, her mouth warm and hungry. Her tongue stroked over his lip, then slipped into his mouth and found his.

And just like that, Grant couldn't remember what they were talking about. The feel of her making that first move, of openly wanting him, blew all his other thoughts out of his mind. He cupped her face and kissed her hard and deep. The satisfied, wanton sound she made in her throat drove Grant to search for more. Her mouth was so fucking perfect. He wanted to rip off her clothes, bury himself inside her, and stay there until they called him back to the ice.

*The ice.*

*Fuck.* He'd had to go and think about that.

He broke the kiss and lifted his head. "Baby…" he said, breathless, "let's talk a minute."

"I don't want to talk." She twisted to reach for the button on his jeans. "I want to use my mouth in other ways."

He grabbed her hand and held on. Hard. If she got her mouth anywhere near his cock, they wouldn't be talking about anything substantial for hours. "I want that too, but I need to know what's going on in that head of yours."

The spark of excitement in her eyes went out. She pulled her hand from his, then rolled to her side again and patted the bed near the laptop. "Come over here and show me how smart you are. I really want to see what you can do with this software."

He stood there, at a loss, while she opened the laptop again. He'd never known a woman who didn't want to talk when she was upset. It was hard to fathom his need to actually elicit the kind of conversation he'd spent his life avoiding, but he cared about Faith. He cared about her life. He cared about what was upsetting her. And he definitely cared if it involved him.

He sat on the edge of the bed and stretched over her, pressing a hand to the mattress. With his fingers, he pushed the laptop out of reach, threaded his fingers with hers, and brought her palm to his lips.

"Are you mad about me going out with Patrick?"

She cut a look at him. "No. Of course not."

Phew. One down. "Did I do something else that made you mad?"

She hesitated. "It's not your fault."

But she broke his gaze and tried to pull her hand back.

*Bingo.*

"Tell me what it is so we can talk about it." Good Lord, he couldn't believe those words were coming out of his mouth.

"It's nothing. It's petty, stupid, small-town bullshit. And it certainly won't matter to you." She lifted her gaze to his again and dragged her hand from his to thread her fingers into his hair and pull him toward her. "I really just want you to make love to me so I can forget all about it."

*Make love?*

That phrase hit him sideways. He'd never thought about sex in that context. But he didn't get a chance to think more about it before she opened to him with that hungry kiss again. And the way she used that delicious mouth of hers made Grant forget everything else. Sweet, sensual, sexual, she'd become one white-hot, luscious erotic masterpiece at the speed of lightning.

When she released his hair to pull at his shirt, Grant put the brakes on. He straightened, breaking her grasp. "Talk first. If it's important enough to upset you, then it's important to me. I don't care if it has to do with Aunt Pearl using chicken wire to fence her pigs, talk to me."

She didn't even twitch a smile at his chicken-wire joke, and unease fluttered in his gut.

Sighing, she brushed her hand across the bedspread, picking at invisible fuzz while Grant stroked her forearm. "It's about the Winter Wonderland Festival. I don't know if you remember much about it when you were a kid, but my dad started it about forty years ago, and he's run it ever since. Even when he was sick, he got out there..."

She trailed off and blinked back tears. Then shook her head. "Anyway, I was all set with the supplies downstairs, and then Natalie came into the store after I'd closed."

Grant listened to Faith's carefully worded, politically correct account of what transpired with Natalie while he'd been enjoying root beer with his brother a block away. But no one knew how to read between the lines like Grant. And he saw Natalie's visit for exactly what it was—an attempt to wedge her way between him and Faith. A way to make Faith feel inferior.

A way to bully her way into a judging position beside Grant. And his teeth were grinding by the time Faith finished the factual details.

"You don't have any obligation to me," she said, now tracing the pattern sewn into the solid comforter with darker thread. "We went into this knowing it was temporary. Neither of us was —I mean is—looking for anything long term. So, you know, if you want to date Natalie, that's up to you."

"Baby, I don't—"

"I know it probably seems ridiculously small-town minded to you," she said, cutting him off with a shake of her head, indicating she didn't want to talk about his relationship—or lack thereof—with Natalie, "but this is my first Christmas without my dad, and this was his favorite h-holiday."

Her voice cracked, and a surge of tears glistened in her eyes again.

Grant's throat grew thick. His gut ached. He couldn't stand to see her hurting.

"I know the town is dressed up for Christmas all year, but Dad truly spent all three hundred sixty-four days preparing for both the festival and the ice-carving contest. The way most kids think about Christmas morning, I think of judging that contest with my dad."

The tears finally slipped over her lashes and slid down her cheeks. Faith sniffled and wiped at one cheek, but Grant rubbed at the other with his thumb before she could get it.

Grant bent over her, collecting her into his arms and cradling her as she cried. With nothing adequate to say, he pressed kisses to her hair instead.

"I'm just not ready to let him go yet," she said, her voice flooded with tears.

"You don't have to," he said quietly, his own throat thick with emotion. "You don't ever have to let him go, baby. You two shared more love in a year than I've had with either of my parents in our entire relationship. Some people just aren't cut out to love the way you and your father could. Letting go of that, of all those amazing memories, of who you've become because of that love, it would be just...tragic."

For the very first time in his entire life, Grant thought he might have the capacity to love like that too. If he connected with the right woman. And he was pretty damn sure that woman was curled in his arms.

After several long moments, her tears ebbed and her breathing eased into a normal rhythm again.

"Thank you," she said softly. "I haven't been able to talk to anyone but Taylor. And she's so busy. Managing this place by myself..." She exhaled. "It's been so hard. So many people don't know how to deal with grief or death. I didn't want to show any kind of weakness or emotion that would make them uncomfortable and keep them from coming into the store. I'm already struggling to stay open."

Grant pulled back and looked directly into Faith's eyes. "You can always talk to me. And I've found a number of ways to help you stay open. I want to talk to you about them. Later, when you're ready."

She nodded and worked up a smile. The movement pushed more tears from her eyes. Grant leaned in and soaked up the trail with kisses, drawing a shaky sigh from Faith that did crazy, twisty things to his heart.

When he drew away, he met her eyes again. "My turn. It's important to me that you know everything Natalie said was bullshit. That woman lives in a fantasyland. I agreed to judge the contest because—"

"Your mother."

"My mother—" they said at the same time.

"I know," she said. "I figured that out thirty seconds into my conversation with Natalie."

Grant explained his family's end game, planning to use

Natalie to draw Grant back to the family business, and the fight they'd had the night he returned home with the Christmas tree.

"The only reason I even stayed in town after that was because I'd already told Dwayne I'd work with his team. If I'd had any idea this festival or the contest was so important to you, I would have set my family straight from the very beginning. And I absolutely *did not* agree to do *anything* with Natalie. If I was forced to spend more than an hour with her, I'd be homicidal."

That got a laugh from Faith and lightened Grant's heart.

"You're the only woman I want, Faith."

This would have been the perfect moment to slip in, *And I really want to continue seeing you.* But given how much turmoil she currently had in her life, he was sure bringing that up now would have drastically increased his chances of losing her. And he didn't want to give her up until he absolutely had to.

So he pulled her in and kissed her the way he'd wanted to kiss her for hours. She dropped her head back and opened to him. The warm touch of her tongue spread fire straight to Grant's groin, and he groaned. Her tears made the kiss salty and real. So honest. So raw. The connection wrapped around Grant's heart and took him under.

He combed one hand into her silky hair and stroked her flat belly with the other, then slid his hand down her silk-covered thigh and moaned into her mouth. Faith kissed him deeper, harder, hungrier. The way she wanted him set him on fire, and he slid his hand up her inner thigh and settled between her legs, cupping her sweet, hot center beneath the silk. Faith groaned, broke the kiss, and pushed her hips into his hand.

"I haven't been able to stop thinking about—"

He kissed her again, hooking his arm around her neck, and pulled her closer. Grant explored her breasts, molding the silk to the bare mounds, teasing her nipples when they hardened beneath his fingers.

But that didn't last, because he needed skin. He needed Faith's smooth, warm, glorious skin, and slipped his hand beneath her tank and lifted it out of the way. Then moved his mouth from her lips to her breasts. And feasted.

The first scrape of his teeth made her arch and whine. She threaded her fingers into his hair and massaged and scratched his scalp as he ate at her. Still, it wasn't enough. He was beginning to believe he'd *never* get enough. While his tongue circled her breast toward her nipple in a teasing spiral, he slipped his hand down her body, beneath the thin silky layers of PJs and panties and right over her sex.

Her pussy was smooth and soft and warm. And when he stroked her plump lips, he found her wet. His growl sounded low and hungry and animalistic.

Faith broke the kiss on a gasp. "God, I love you touching me. Is that weird? I can't believe how good that—" Another gasp. A high-pitched "Mmmm. Grant..."

He lifted his mouth from her breast and watched the building pleasure wash over her face. "That's hot. That's an incredible turn-on. That's sexy as hell. That is *not* weird."

"Oh good," she breathed. "Because you are so *fucking* good at it."

The woman made him feel as amazing as a packed stadium on a stellar night. And he pulled out every trick he knew to draw shivers and moans and gasps from her lips. "Open for me, Faith."

When she dropped one knee to the side, baring herself for his touch, a hat-trick-worthy rush pumped through his blood. He stroked, he teased, he thrust, he stretched, he rubbed. He wet his fingers and strayed toward her backside, which earned him an extra pulse of her hips. And when she finally couldn't take any more, he pushed deep with his two middle fingers and rubbed her inner wall while he used his thumb to massage circles over her clit.

And the sight of her climbing to that peak was so beautiful, Grant purposely made it a slow climb. A steady climb. To give him time to get his mouth back on her breasts. To absorb more of those sexy sounds she made that exploded in his groin like firecrackers.

But before long, she was rocking into his hand, seeking out more pressure. And damn, that was so hot. By the time morning broke, he planned to have her riding his mouth like an expert.

"Grant...Grant...Grant...Ah..."

Her muscles contracted and pulled her into a curl. Her pussy spilled juice over his fingers and shuddered around them. And she continued to shake and shiver for long moments afterward.

When her muscles softened and her eyes closed, Grant drew his hand from her sex and used his other hand to lift her head so he could kiss her, slow and sweet. "You are so fucking gorgeous when you come."

"God, that's good," she murmured. "I love what you do to me."

Now *that* was the most promising thing he'd heard all night. "That's good, baby." He tugged her tank off over her head, shimmied her pants and panties down her hips and thighs, letting her kick them off her feet, and grabbed for his wallet in the back pocket of his jeans. "Because I love doing it to you. And I love what doing it to you does to me."

His cock was throbbing mad that it didn't get in on that sweet action.

She was still lying on her side, now with her arm curled under her head, her eyes closed. Her cheeks were flushed, and her pretty pale hair spilled across the dark sheets.

"You're not going to fall asleep on me, are you?" He grabbed the condom with his teeth and worked his jeans open with his free hand. "I have lots more ways to make you feel good."

"I'm definitely not falling asleep." She was still talking. That was a good sign, even though she sounded like she'd fall asleep any second. "I'm getting my second wind."

He chuckled as he rolled on the condom, then stroked all her luscious skin. He wanted to get naked and rub all over her, and he would, but he had a more urgent need to bond with her after the emotion they'd shared. Somehow he felt like loving her now was sort of sealing the deal and holding that moment between them.

Stupid, maybe. But he needed her. He really, really needed to claim her. Right now.

She pushed up on her elbow, moved toward the middle of the bed, and reached over to nudge Grant's laptop aside—giving Grant one killer view of her beautiful ass. He pressed a knee between her thighs and stroked his hands up her legs, over her cheeks, her ribs, her shoulders, her neck, and threaded one hand into her hair, using the soft mass to gently lift and turn her head to cover her mouth with his.

Faith licked into his mouth with her eyes open and hot. She lifted her ass, rocked against his hips, and hummed with desire. His need skyrocketed, and he conveyed that with his mouth. Faith returned the fierce kisses and gentle bites, lifting to her elbows and arching her back to rub him harder with that gorgeous ass.

She pulled back to whisper, "Inside me, Grant. I need you."

The words created an implosion in his chest, crumbling any defenses that might have remained. He positioned himself, then tightened his hand and held her gaze as he pushed inside. Everything about the way she received him turned him inside out. The way her mouth dropped open. The way her eyes rolled back until they closed. The way she rose and eased onto him, as if she couldn't get all of him fast enough. The long, slow moan that rolled from her throat as he filled her.

And finally, her verbal approval. "*Oh, yes.* Yes, yes, *yes.*" Until he couldn't get any deeper and she groaned, "*God, yes.*"

And when he refastened his grip in her hair so he could hold her gaze as he thrust, her sounds of approval drove his hips harder and harder.

She pulled her knees under her and arched her back. Grant's position and the strength of his thrusts pushed her head to the mattress. Her hands curled into the bedspread, and she used the tension created from the weight of her body to push herself back and into his thrust.

"I can't...believe the things...I let you do...to me," she said, panting as she rose to climax. "I can't believe how...good it is."

Grant couldn't believe how sexy she was. Or how lucky he'd gotten in finding her.

As her passion rose, she pushed harder, demanding more force. Grant loved the way she gave herself over to whatever her body wanted. He released her hair and took a more centered position behind her, allowing him to thrust harder, hammer deeper, and within seconds, Faith shattered with a scream and a whimper, her muscles quivering uncontrollably through the letdown.

Wicked satisfaction swamped him. He stayed deep inside her while she recovered, stroking his hands up and down her back and hips.

When she stirred, he withdrew. He shucked his shirt and pants in seconds and sat on the bed, collecting Faith into his arms, and spreading her thighs to straddle his lap. And easily reentered her as she settled into position.

They spent long moments kissing and touching and just staring at each other. Grant had never done this with a woman, and he couldn't get enough of it with Faith. But his body's need soon took control of the steering wheel. And there was something different between them now. Something new, something deep. Some kind of understanding he couldn't put words to.

But he was sure they were on the same page. In fact, he'd never been more sure of anything.

And as he pulled his legs under him and used his thighs to drive into her, Faith wrapped her arms around his shoulders, pressed her forehead to his, and held his gaze steadily, lovingly, until she finally peaked again. Grant let go at the same moment and kissed her as they tumbled into bliss together. He was sure he'd never felt anything more perfect in his life.

Faith rested her head against his chest, and her warm breath bathed his skin. Grant sat back on his heels and stroked her hair, her back, her shoulders. When his feet started to tingle, he kissed her head and murmured, "I'm fuckin' crazy about you, Faith."

She didn't answer and a trickle of heat coursed through his gut. Alarm? Hurt? It was so foreign he couldn't even identify it. Maybe it was just too soon to be voicing it. She really did have a lot of other things, more important things, to think about. Still...he didn't like this feeling.

He pushed up on his knees and found her far heavier than she'd been just minutes before. He cocked his head to look down at her face and found her eyes closed. The stricture in his chest loosened a little.

"Faith?"

No answer. Not even a flicker of her lashes.

He grinned and tried one more time. "What do you think? Still want to work on that video tonight?"

He got nothin'.

The last of the unease inside him vanished. He chuckled, stroked her hair, and kissed her head again. "Don't worry, baby. I'm here to back you now."

And—*damn*—that felt so good.

# 14

Faith set up the last table inside the covered arena at the county fairgrounds and shook it to test for stability. The ice sculptures could weigh hundreds of pounds, and she didn't want this year to be the first year a table gave out and ruined the contest for someone.

When the heavy-duty table held, Faith smiled and ran her hand over the wood her father had handcrafted for this event. But that brought a flurry of other thoughts and emotions. First her mind turned to Natalie and her curt call to Faith early that morning to tell Faith that since she was being so unreasonable, Natalie would forego judging for the greater good so that Holly would benefit.

"Martyr," Faith muttered, running her finger over one of the many scars in the table. But she was still ashamed of herself for coming down to Natalie's level. "That won't happen next year..."

Faith trailed off, realizing next year was one big question mark. She might not be able to make the store profitable enough to hold on to. She might be somewhere completely different, starting over. Alone. No Taylor, no Caleb, none of the people from Holly whom she'd known all her life.

*No Grant.*

Faith sighed and started moving methodically among the tables to double-check the extension cord connections.

Her cell rang, and she smiled a little, looking forward to the sound of Grant's voice. As she pulled it from her back pocket, their night flooded back to her. He'd slowly been edging his way into her heart since he showed up in town. But last night he'd impressed the hell out of her. How open he'd been when she'd told him about Natalie. How reassuring he'd been about his feelings for her. How receptive he'd been of her emotions.

And the way he'd made love to her after... God, it had been the most beautiful night of her life. Passionate. Loving. Intense. She'd never felt as connected to another human being as she'd felt to Grant last night, looking into his eyes.

She looked at the screen and saw Taylor's name. Which made her think of how Grant had been gone when she woke up this morning. And made her wonder if he'd felt it too. And that it had scared him into pulling away.

"Hey," she answered. "I thought you were going over the books with Grant."

"I'm headed there now, but I called because—"

"Weren't you supposed to do that this morning?" It was the reason he'd given her when he'd texted later in the morning to tell her he couldn't help her set up.

"No, he said he had something else to do this morning and pushed it back."

A pang of hurt pulled hard at the center of Faith's body. She winced and pressed a hand to her forehead. "I see."

"No, I don't think you do. I just figured out what he was doing."

Now dread joined the hurt. But Taylor sounded excited, and she would never be excited about Faith getting hurt. "And?"

"Your Christmas Light Fantasia is up on YouTube. It looks incredible. It's adorable and funny and informative. And the final result is a-freaking-mazing."

She grinned, excited. "Really?" He'd spent the morning editing her video? "But...I didn't get around to narrating..."

"Grant did. And he's *really* good. He's got a sexy, professional voice, yet he's got a really straightforward way about explaining things, and he's funny. Must be all those interviews he does with the media all the time."

He did media interviews? She really needed to learn more about hockey and the NHL and... She shook her head. Yeah. Maybe in her spare time.

"Wow," she said. "That's amazing." She couldn't stop smiling—even though she knew without any doubt her heart was going to shatter when he left. Which reminded her that she only had a couple of days left with him before he returned to DC to reenter hockey season.

"It is," Taylor agreed. "But what's really amazing—are you sitting down?"

Faith slid her butt onto the nearest table. "I am now."

"You've already gotten one hundred and twenty *thousand* views."

Faith's mouth dropped open. "*What?*"

"But it gets better."

"How?"

"He went online, found the components necessary to put the whole thing together, listed them, and linked to them on the Home Depot website."

Faith laughed. "Well, that's great for Home Depot, but it doesn't do anything for me."

"It does when you have an affiliate account."

"I don't—"

"Yes, you do. Grant set one up for you."

Her mind swirled. She was still high on the number of views of the video alone. "What? How?"

"This is the beauty of living in a small town, girlie. You bank at Old Town Bank, which is managed by Betty Fleur. Betty's son, Hank, played hockey with Grant from the time they could skate until they left for college. Grant's parents also keep their money locally and bank there. So when Grant went in and told her what he wanted to do, Betty did everything short of jumping over the teller counter to help him hook up your bank account to the affiliate account. But I hear she did it without giving him access to your account information. Now, just so you know, the funds for affiliates don't go in for thirty days, so whatever you see in your Home Depot account won't be deposited into your bank account for a month."

Faith pressed a hand to her heart. "But...how do you know all this?"

"Faith, seriously? The same way I know his car's been outside your shop *two nights in a row*."

She said the last with a how-could-you-not-tell-me you're-gonna-hear-about-this-later tone. Which meant that between friends and family members, Taylor had probably gotten that information from half a dozen different sources, vetted it, and pieced together a very accurate story.

"Oh my God." Her stomach jittered so hard, she felt sick. She dropped her hand from her heart to her stomach, then gripped the table edge. "That's..." Tears welled in her eyes. "Oh my God."

"I hope he's good in bed, girlie, 'cause that boy is a winner in every other way. I just pulled up to the store. I'll call you if I find out more, but I have a feeling he'll be seeing you before I do, so you'll probably already have the scoop by then."

Taylor didn't bother to say good-bye before she disconnected. And Faith lowered her phone, staring at it in awe. She couldn't begin to fathom having anyone think of her so...

unselfishly. Anyone but her father. And even he hadn't been able to do that for years. Not since he'd gotten sick.

Faith didn't know how to respond to such a kind act. How did she go about thanking someone for something like that? It wasn't just the time he'd spent working on the video and setting up the accounts. It was doing it for her when he knew she couldn't do it for herself, yet needed it so badly. It was his ability to think ten steps ahead of her and anticipate her needs, then fill them while she was still struggling moment to moment. It was the sheer fact that he'd not only listened to her, but he'd *heard* her and then taken that next step and actually made something *happen* for her.

She wished Taylor wasn't with him. Faith wanted to leave here right now and find him. Beyond wrapping him in a bear hug and kissing him until he couldn't breathe, she didn't know what she'd do to thank him. Because she already gave herself over to him completely on a nightly basis and would continue to do so until he returned to his real world.

"That's an awful deep look of concentration."

The male voice startled her out of her thoughts. Dwayne strolled beneath the arena's cover, hands in his pockets, a big grin on his face. Faith's mind shifted gears. "Hey, there." She turned to face him. "That's the biggest smile I've seen on your face in a while."

"Grant's had that effect on a lot of people in town." He came up beside Faith and slipped up onto the table next to her. She loved the way no one even thought to question her father's craftsmanship. "You should see the effect he's had on the boys. He's given that whole team an infusion of pure energy. They're working twice as hard and having twice as much fun doing it. I'm really glad you and Grant became friends. You're both orphans in a way. Both such good people. I love it when good things happen to good people."

He sighed happily and looked around. "Where is that boy?

He told me he had to move practice until this afternoon because he was helping you set up."

"He was going to, but something else came up that he needed to take care of."

Dwayne nodded. "Well, I'm glad he got home even if he did have to deal with his family while he was here. That didn't turn out all bad. And it gave him a break from all that baloney he lives with."

Faith shook her head confused. She couldn't tell if Dwayne was talking about his family here or... "Baloney." She smiled, remembering how her dad loved that phrase. "That reminds me of Dad."

"Yeah. I miss that man. We knew what baloney was. These young men, they haven't figured it out yet."

"And that would be...?" she asked.

"All the smoke and mirrors around him up there in DC. All the ESPN interviews, the newspaper articles, *Sports Illustrated* features. Money, power, and women—they're the three common denominators in the downfalls of all great men. In Grant's case, power comes in two forms—money and fame. He's already got more money than he'll ever spend in his lifetime, and I always see him with a different woman on his arm at all those events he attends for the team to please charities, sponsors, owners, and managers. And each of those women is just as rich, beautiful, and powerful as Grant."

Dwayne waved it away like he was swatting a fly. "It's all baloney. It's not real. And when it all disappears...well...if that's all you had, you're left with nothing. At least nothing substantial."

Faith was still trying to absorb all Dwayne had just told her about Grant in the span of two minutes. It opened up a whole new perspective on both the man and his life back in DC.

Her excitement had been relegated to a corner, and her heart dropped a little lower in her chest.

"Ah," she said, as if it all made sense now, when in fact, the more she learned, the less she understood. "*That* baloney."

Dwayne chuckled and patted her knee. "What can I help you with, darlin'?"

"Uh..." Faith refocused and looked around. "Actually, nothing. I'm done with all the big stuff. Now I'm just wandering around double-checking things."

Dwayne gave her a long sweet hug. "Your daddy'd be proud of his little girl."

Unfortunately, Faith seriously doubted it. "Thanks, Dwayne."

# 15

Grant had taken pages and pages of notes from his hour-long talk with Taylor. A talk he'd realized within the first ten minutes would take weeks, maybe months, to adequately flesh out and understand.

"So, you can see here"—Taylor pointed to one of the several spreadsheets she'd brought over—"I have several revenue streams that I monitor at all times. That way, I can tell where I need to either concentrate or cut, change, whatever."

They were sitting at a small desk in the basement that Faith used as an office, and he'd been cooped up there long before Taylor had come by, trying to figure out a better way of running the store so Faith could make a livable wage. And he'd realized a couple of important things.

The first was that if she wasn't ready to give up something as intangible as judging an ice-carving contest, she sure as hell wouldn't be ready to do what Grant really thought she ought to do, which was get rid of the store and do something she really loved. The second was, if she couldn't do the first, she sure wouldn't be open to the complexity of trying to continue a relationship with Grant.

The only bright spot was Taylor and this niche she'd carved out in what seemed to be a market that wasn't only thriving, but growing.

Grant shook his head, still staring at the numbers on her spreadsheet. "Don't take this wrong, Taylor, but, if I'm understanding this right, you make a shitload of money for talking about really stupid-ass shit."

To Grant's relief, Taylor laughed.

"That doesn't bother me because you're not my target audience," she told him. "And my target audience finds pushing a three-inch disc of vulcanized rubber around an ice rink with a stick while brawling with a bunch of other guys some really stupid-ass shit."

Grant grinned. "Good point."

"If you use this as a template, you could, in theory, simply change the topics and have Faith film how-to segments the same way." She leaned back. "For example, instead of a post about how to design your planner for maximum efficiency, Faith would create a post about how to design your *garage workbench* for maximum efficiency. And instead of posting links to all the pens, papers, stickers, and stamps I used in the process, she would do what you did with her Christmas lights video—ingenious and incredibly sweet, by the way—and link to all the wood, screws, nails, glue, tools, and paint *she used* to complete the process."

Grant nodded, his mind spinning with ideas. Visions of how this could grow. "Okay. I see it."

"Another category she could look into to build revenue streams and gain sponsors would be product reviews. For example, instead of my review on a new version of the Erin Condren Life Planner, Faith would review the newest version of the newly released DeWalt sliding miter saw."

Grant nodded. "Yep. I get it."

"Her blog posts will contain photos and videos that feed

into all her social media outlets. In turn, all her social media posts will track back to her blog posts. And she'll use a master link system that feeds all clicks through her affiliate links, so that no matter how a person finds their way to Home Depot or Lowes or wherever from her post, Faith will always be compensated for a sale."

Taylor lifted her hand, index finger poised. "Now, once she has a following, she can start reaching out to companies to solicit advertising, sponsorships, and even partnerships. And if she wants to, she can create an online store where a person could go to buy everything they need to complete a project she's demonstrated. She could even put together kits at cost and sell them at retail. Really, the sky is the limit here."

"This is amazing."

"She doesn't even have to be an actress or have special equipment to produce these videos. As long as her space, presentation, and speaking are professional and easy to understand, she could use her phone to do it. Though, come to think of it, hers probably doesn't have enough memory."

"That's okay. I'm leaving the camera, software, and laptop with her."

"Really? She agreed to that?"

He looked over and found Taylor's brows snapped together in disbelief.

"No." He smiled, but it was subdued. "She doesn't know it. I'm going to stuff them under her bed before I go. You get to be the bearer of that news."

Taylor smirked. "Gee, thanks."

"What are friends for?"

"But seriously, that's incredibly sweet of you."

Grant shook his head. In his world, that equipment cost less than his bar tab after buying drinks for the team when he'd been chosen MVP for the night. "I know she'd throw a fit if I tried to give it to her outright."

"You got her figured out fast."

He grinned. "She's not exactly complicated. Proud, loyal, and mildly frustrating, maybe. But not complicated."

Taylor's smile was warm. "She's amazing, isn't she?"

He closed his eyes on a laugh. "Fucking incredible."

Taylor reached out and squeezed his forearm. The affectionate gesture told Grant he'd passed the best-friend test. He only wished that was the biggest of the roadblocks facing him and Faith.

"Actually, the most popular tutorials are those that relate to the average Joe," Taylor said. "And as you can see by the popularity of the segment you put up for her, her looks and sweet personality will be as big a hit on camera as they are in town." She propped her elbow on the desk and rested her head in her hand. "Now, let's talk about exactly how you got that video to shoot up in the views so fast."

He lifted his brows. "You just said—"

"Uh-uh." She made a cutting gesture in the air between them. "You're talking to the expert here. I know that video had help. I want to know what it is."

"Don't tell Faith."

"Can't promise."

He sighed. "Okay, don't tell her right away. Let her have the excitement for a little while. She needs a little hope in her life."

"Wow." Taylor shook her head. "You're almost too good to be true." She narrowed her eyes. "If I find out you're married, I'm going to hunt you down and cut off your balls."

"Whoa." He laughed the word and put his hands up. "I'm *not* married."

She pointed at him. "You've been warned. All right, dish."

"I posted the video, then sent an email to all the guys on the team and asked them to share it on social media."

"Oh." Taylor's eyes glazed over as thoughts churned in her head. "*Oh.*"

"Yeah."

"And you're a freaking marketing genius too?" More narrow-eyed looks. "I'm watching you."

"I have been warned," he echoed, smiling. "So, everything we just talked about gets you here?" Grant tapped the mid-six-figure number at the bottom of Taylor's income sheet for the prior year.

"It does. Isn't that crazy?"

"Why didn't she do this a long time ago? When she saw it was working for you, why didn't she start doing it then?"

"Her dad was pretty old-fashioned. Believed business should be between two people, face-to-face, and she didn't want to upset him. Besides, she had too much going on. This is a serious time suck, one that doesn't immediately pay off, and she was taking complete care of her dad and running the store. Toward the end, her father had to get angry for her to finally allow Hospice to come once a day."

Grant dropped back in his chair, blew out a long breath, his gaze on the papers that signified limitless opportunities for Faith. A chance at the freedom she should have had in life.

"God, I'm so damned excited about this for her."

"Right? I'm really excited you got her started. Between the store, my work, and Caleb, we've both been so busy, we haven't been able to work out a time to get it together. Again, this is no Holy Grail in marketing. No perfect system. And there's a huge amount of work involved, not to mention an incredibly steep learning curve. The results yielded are based on the work put in—"

"You get amazing results."

"Because I've already climbed those mountains. So, I will be doing my best to cut her learning curve into a very flat plateau."

Grant nodded, but his brain kept repeating: *"And she can do it from anywhere."*

His cell rang. He reached for his back pocket. "Hope that's

Faith. She was going to call when she was ready to put up the tables." But it wasn't. He glanced at Taylor. "My agent."

"Oh, okay." She stood. "We're done. I'll get all this from Faith later."

Grant stood too. "Thanks so much. Faith's lucky to have such a great friend."

Once Taylor climbed the basement stairs, Grant answered, "Hey, Nick."

"Hey, how's Twisted Christmas?"

That was only one of his agent's nicknames for Grant's hometown. But Grant wasn't in the mood for Nick's wry humor. "Did they clear me?"

"Not yet."

He was both frustrated and grateful. "Why not? This is taking freaking forever."

"Danbar's on vacation in the Caribbean."

Doctor Danbar was the last signature Grant needed on his release forms. "Fucking A." He threaded his hand into his hair. "This is ridiculous."

"Relax. He'll be back tomorrow, and I've already talked to Max," Nick said, referencing the team's manager. "You'll go right back to first line when you hit the ice. Hey, I've got something that will cheer you right up—the perfect way to get you out of that backward little Christmas town and into a place where we know how to do it right."

Grant squeezed his eyes closed and dropped his hand. "What are you talking about?"

"You're going to a special event at the sight of the National Christmas Tree and the VIP After-Party hosted by the National Park Foundation. Ted made a big donation to the Foundation this year," he said, referring to the Rough Riders' owner, Theodore Hennessey, "and he and Fiona are in France for the holiday. So he's sending you, Croft, Savage, Donovan, Hendrix, Andrade, and Lawless to represent the team. This is an awesome photo op for you to get your face back into the light after being out eight weeks."

"Ah, wow, Nick…" His chest tightened. His skin crawled. "You know, I don't—"

"They're putting special lights on the tree, selling gourmet hot cider, hot chocolate, roasted chestnuts, shit like that. They've even got *Giselle Diamond* singing Christmas carols. Can you believe that? I mean, I guess I can. She's a huge proponent of charity, and the proceeds benefit the US Sports Foundation. I'm sure when she heard that, she jumped on board. And, evidently, the president's daughters are huge Diamond fans."

This just kept getting worse. "The president is going to be there?"

"It's *his* Christmas Tree. In front of *his* house. But he's just showing his face to raise his numbers in the polls. There will be other local celebrities there and a portion of the donations will go directly to the US Hockey Foundation…"

*Fuuuuck.* Grant dropped his head back. He was all for charity. Sometimes felt like he participated in more charity events than hockey games. But this one day, he really wanted to spend with Faith.

"Nick—" Grant tried to break in.

"I've already got all of you guys the *hottest* dates on the planet. You can thank me later. You're escorting Bridgette Ferreira."

Grant winced. Bridgette was okay, and if he hadn't met Faith, he'd be happy to return to the sheets with the model-turned-broadcaster, but now…no. The only woman he wanted in his sheets was Faith.

"The event is, of course, tomorrow," Nick said, "and since you're in Nowhere, USA, I had to book you a crazy flight schedule to get you out of Twisted Christmas and into DC in time for the event. You're leaving tonight."

"Just hold on." Grant rubbed a hand over his face and

started to pace. "Remember why I'm here in the first place? Ted was the one busting my ass about spending too much time with women like Bridgette. Ted was the one who forced me to choose something 'meaningful' to do with the rest of my rehabilitation time. So, I'm here, doing that. He can't just wiggle his nose like a fuckin' witch and bring me back to DC whenever he wants."

"Uhhh, yeah. He can. He pays your salary. These events are in your contract. I thought you'd be offering to name your first-born after me when I gave you the news."

Grant dropped his head back and glared at the ceiling. *Noooooooooooo!*

"I'm here for the kids, Nick. I don't want to bail on them." It was true, but he was picturing Faith in his mind. "This is charity too. I'm bringing in a lot of money for my high school team. Just tell him I can't make it and pick someone else."

"Dude," Nick said in his what-the-fuck-do-you-mean-no? tone. "What's wrong with you? It's Christmas and all the other guys just finished five fucking grueling away games. One of the reasons Ted chose you guys is because all of you either live locally in DC or don't have kids. And may I stress *Ted chose you.*"

Which translated to *Go if you want another offer when your current contract runs out.*

Grant hung his head. "Right, sorry. My parents are making me crazy. And I promised these kids—"

"This isn't negotiable. This is contractual. And if you're not on that plane, you're in breach of that contract. All you've got to do is be seen, get that pretty face on the news tomorrow night at the event. Sign some autographs and get a few photos with celebrities at one of the parties you go to while you're in town. Make Ted happy. Ticket's in your email."

# 16

Faith's mind kept winding its way back around to "what if" and "maybe" as she tested the last string of lights illuminating the ice-carving stations. She'd already packed up her gear and stored it in one of the storage sheds on-site. In a few days, she'd come do this all over again—in reverse.

By then, Grant would be gone. He'd come and gone from her life in what seemed like a flash, yet he'd left an indelible mark on her—heart and soul. She couldn't help but wonder how long it would take her to get over him. How long it would take her to move on. Or whether she'd ever find a man like him to love again.

Love...?

She thought about that a few seconds, trying on that new description.

Not only did the feeling fit immediately, the rightness of it wrapped her in warmth and joy.

And those damn maybes and what-ifs filled her mind again.

When Faith flipped the switch and all the bulbs in the last row of lights glowed, she knew she was done. Her first year setting up without her dad. Without anyone.

Now she knew she could do it on her own.

Instead of that knowledge relaxing her or bolstering her, it depressed her. She was tired of doing everything on her own. Her mind drifted toward the puzzle of continuing to see Grant when he returned to DC. She spun the pieces in her mind, tried to make them fit. When they didn't, she took out those pieces and tried others. Still no good.

HER PHONE CHIMED, and she smiled, anticipating a text from him. But when she pulled her cell from her pocket, she found a new email. From Natalie.

"Ugh." Dread and guilt twined as she tapped it open, wondering what snarky comment Natalie had delivered now.

But no words filled the email. Just photos. Image after image after image of Grant with different women. Faith's gut tightened automatically, as if fending off a punch.

They all looked like paparazzi pics or event photos. None were provocative, but they all clearly displayed Grant as an attentive, affectionate half of a couple.

With her stomach aching, Faith shored up a framework for her thoughts. She knew Grant was a player. A player was exactly the kind of man she'd been trying out when she'd gone into this fling. He'd never made promises. Never led her to believe anything in his life would change once he left Holly for DC or any other city. He owed her nothing.

But, no, that didn't magically erase the pain.

She blew out a slow breath and focused on the single line of text below each image.

*Miriam Birovski, CFO, Birovski Vodka.*

*Daphne Johnson, corporate attorney, Oracle.*

*Tiffany Shapiro, model.*

*Bridgette Ferreira, model, broadcaster.*

Faith continued scrolling, scanning over a dozen

photographs, names, and titles while the uncomfortable tightness beneath her ribs became a stabbing pain.

At the bottom, Natalie's parting message hammered every one of Faith's insecurities home: *You'll never belong.*

She forced her eyes closed and turned off her screen. None of that mattered, because this wasn't permanent. This wasn't *real.* This was a fling.

"There you are." Grant's voice startled her, and she pivoted toward him. He was smiling, but not in that light, happy way she'd come to love. "I thought you were going to call me to help you set up the tables."

He wore his parka and jeans. His knit hat was covered with snow.

"You were already spending all that extra time looking at my books and working on a marketing plan with Taylor," she said, starting in his direction.

When he was beneath the arena's cover, he pulled off his hat and ran a hand through his hair while he looked around at Faith's setup. "Man, this looks *fantastic.*"

She smiled and went to him. He was still hers for a few more days. So she slid her hands underneath his jacket and over the soft cotton of his tee and all the warm muscle beneath. And she hugged him tight. "*You're* fantastic." She smiled up at him. "Thank you for finishing the video for me. And getting it up online. And...just...being so all-around amazing."

"Hold off on that assessment." He wrapped her in his arms, framed her face with one hand, and kissed her. And even the kiss was different. A steady press of his lips that lingered, as if he didn't want to let go. It tugged at her already aching heartstrings.

When he pulled back and looked into her eyes, she knew this wasn't going to be something she wanted to hear. She laid her hand against his chest. "What's wrong?"

He wrapped one big, warm hand around hers. "I just got a call from my agent."

Faith tensed against another blow.

"God, I'm so sorry to do this to you, Faith." He exhaled heavily. "He booked me for an event tomorrow, and I can't get out of it. These appearances are in my contract, and I can't bum it off on anyone else, because the guys who can go are already going. The others are married with kids and spending the night with their families."

She nodded, but she stood on the edge of a cliff with a very long fall waiting. "Where's the event?"

"DC."

Exactly what she feared, but she tried like hell to hold it together. "So you won't be here for"—*Christmas*—"the contest?"

He looked down at their joined hands and shook his head. "I'm sorry, baby. I have to leave tonight."

*Tonight?*

That news hit her hard. Really hard.

She wasn't ready.

"Oh, wow." Tears pushed at her eyes out of nowhere, and she let her gaze fall to his chest. "O-okay. Sure. I understand. You have to go where they want you, right?" She managed a soft bubble of laughter. "I'm lucky we met at all. If you hadn't hurt yourself and been benched, you would never have come home for Christmas and..."

*And I wouldn't be standing here with my hopes falling ten stories.*

Wild flutters of panic attacked, and Faith had the crazy urge to grab hold of him. She forced herself to look at this rationally. Logically. Tried to put it in perspective. They'd known each other only a couple of weeks. Their lives couldn't be more different.

This was good. A quick, clean end. Better than dragging it out, getting more attached. Right?

She looked up just as he combed his hand through her hair and kissed her again. The move was so sweet, so familiar, so comforting, it killed her to think of losing him. She cupped his cheek and tried to memorize the feel of his lips.

But he pulled back too soon. "I've arranged for Dwayne to step in for me so you won't have to judge with Natalie—"

"You know, I've been thinking about that." The words spilled from her mouth in a now-or-never, throw-caution-to-the-wind gamble. Because in that moment, she realized she wanted to hold on to Grant more than she wanted to hold on to her ghosts from the past. More than she wanted to hold on to her anger. "I overreacted about judging. The stress has my emotions swinging all over the place. I don't need to judge the contest." She smiled, trying to trick herself into easing the intensity crushing her chest. "Once you've seen a couple thousand ice sculptures, you've seen 'em all, right?"

His brow furrowed a little, creating a vertical line. "But—"

"And I've been thinking about what you said last night too. Memories live in here." She patted his chest. "Not in any event. Not in any physical object or geographical location. So no matter what I do or where I go, I'll always have my dad with me. I don't need this contest or the store or even Holly to hold on to him."

Grant's expression lightened, but he still looked concerned. "Baby, you've been through a lot, and I think you're going to discover awesome things about yourself in the next few months." He stroked his knuckles over her jaw, his gaze soft on hers. "But I hope you know that I think you're already amazing."

"I think you're amazing too." Faith took a deep breath and dove in with hope sparking in her heart. She'd opened the door for him to step through, if that was what he wanted. "So what's this event they have you doing?"

He seemed more interested in tucking her hair perfectly

behind her ear than the event. "Some special thing they're doing tomorrow at the National Christmas Tree."

"Wait, is that... That's not..." But she couldn't think of any other event. "The one in front of the White House?" When he didn't correct her, she added, "The one that *the president* and his family attend?"

He chuckled at her awe, reminding Faith how sheltered her life was in small-town USA.

"Yeah." He shook his head, unimpressed. "I've met him before. I know it seems like a big deal, and the first time, yeah, I guess it was cool, but it's really not that...I don't know...special, I guess."

Not special to him, she thought, because he was so out of her league, maybe.

"I'm sorry," he added after a second. "That made me sound...self-important. What I meant was that he's actually accessible to more people than you would imagine. And he happens to be a fan of the Rough Riders. If he were a fan of the Fliers or the Islanders or something, I never would have met him."

He sighed with a shake of his head and rubbed his eyes. "I think the more I talk, the worse I sound. I guess, like you with ice sculptures, once you've seen a few tree lightings, you've seen 'em all. And with these kinds of events, it's never just one thing. There's always a pre-party and an after-party, and an after-after-party... The socializing is endless. But I need to schmooze with the media to talk up my return to the game. There's a lot more to hockey at this level than just hockey."

"Evidently." And it only made her think of all those gorgeous, cultured women he took to all those non-hockey events. "Who knew?"

He huffed a laugh. "Right?"

That uncomfortable tightness gathered at the center of her chest again. "But still, that's an opportunity most people will go their whole lives without ever experiencing. And it sounds pretty damn swanky."

"I guess." He lifted a shoulder. "I know it makes me sound ungrateful, and I'm not, but I don't want to go."

She didn't want him to go either. And if he had to go, she wished he'd ask her to go with him. She'd done everything but invite herself. But she was starting to realize that idea was straight out of a fairy tale.

"The event will be televised. You might see me on the edge of the crowd, standing with a gaggle of other scruffy guys." He slid his arms around her waist, then lifted his mouth in a half smile. "Will you watch?"

Ice water doused Faith's last flicker of hope. Natalie had been right. Grant wouldn't ask her to come with him, because she didn't belong in that world. His *real* world. Holly was his temporary fantasyland. Hockey and all the locations it took him—that was Grant's *real* world. The world with all the lights and cameras, autographs and interviews, dates with supermodels and CFOs, and meeting the freaking president of the United States.

And Faith, small-town hardware store owner on the verge of bankruptcy, not only didn't belong, she couldn't fit in no matter what she did or how she tried.

The reality of that hurt in a way she couldn't put into words.

"You bet." She forced a smile, patted his chest, and stepped out of the circle of his arms. "I'm going to let Natalie know she'll be judging the contest on her own, and I'll be sure to surf cable tomorrow night to see if I can catch sight of you."

He looked disappointed and a little lost. Twisting his wrist, he glanced at his watch, then dropped his arm. But he didn't ask her to come. Didn't suggest plans when he returned. And she couldn't bear dragging out this good-bye any longer.

"Don't be late," she said with a smile and shooing gesture as she walked backward. The more space she created between them, the less likely she would be to lunge after him when he turned to go. "You shouldn't keep the president of the United States waiting."

"I, um...I looked through all Taylor's numbers and jotted down a rough sketch of a similar plan for you. It's on your desk."

"Great. I'll look it over tonight. Thanks again. For everything."

"I think it's a great idea," he added, still not moving.

She nodded, kissed the fingertips of one glove, and used that hand to wave to him. "Safe travels, Grant Saber."

And she turned away, put her gaze on the dirty snow path leading to the parking lot, and kept her head down and her mind focused on getting one foot in front of the other.

# 17

Grant was fucking miserable.

Everything about this gig had been as tedious as he'd expected—the flights to get here, the traffic from the airport, the wardrobe fitting for a tux, Bridgette's pawing at the cocktail party beforehand, and now, he and his teammates were standing in a brutally cold DC wind that created a thirty-four-degrees-feels-like-seven-degrees situation just to watch some lights turn on.

The only light in this dark cloud had been the performance by Giselle Diamond. Despite the cold and the wind, she'd put on an outstanding show. Her voice silenced the massive audience until the end of a song when the applause and cheering rose to ear-splitting levels. That had been the only part of tonight he was sorry Faith had missed.

*Faith.*

He took a covert glance at his phone to check for texts, emails, or voice messages. Still nothing. That knot of fear digging into his ribs tightened a little more.

"Would it be...how you say...vulgar, to ask how the fuck we got here?" Andre Kristoff asked in his thick Russian accent.

"It's called rude," Beckett Croft, one of the team's best defensemen answered. "And sometimes, you just gotta say what you gotta say. What I want to know is how the fuck do we get out?"

"Better question," Tate Donovan said under his breath, "is how to shut you guys up so we don't get *kicked out*."

"Whose idea was it to bring the fuckin' Boy Scout along?" Rafe Savage cut a look at his best friend since childhood and his current teammate on the Rough Riders. "I've got my eye on a couple of sweet pieces of ass from the cocktail party, and I'm taking at least one of them home tonight. So if you plan on acting as the goddamned hall monitor, stay the fuck away from me."

"I'm going to repeat that to you the next time you call me from jail looking for someone to bail out your skanky ass," Tate shot back, using a high-pitched girlie voice to repeat, "Stay the fuck away from me."

Normally, Grant found Rafe's and Tate's bitching entertaining. Tonight, he found nothing entertaining. Absolutely nothing. He'd only been away from Faith for about thirty hours and all he could focus on was the hollow ache in his gut.

Rafe pulled his jacket tighter against the bitter DC wind. "Bet he wouldn't talk so damn long if he were out here instead of up there, shielded and warm. Fucker."

"Say that a little louder," Beckett told him. "Maybe to that Secret Service agent or bodyguard or whoever the hell that is on your right."

"It's a free fucking country." He met the steely gaze of the noted agent or guard. "Isn't that right? Sir."

The man didn't respond but took in every last detail of their group before scanning the crowd again.

"Would you guys shut up?" Hendrix said from behind them, his arms crossed, jacket pulled up around his ears. He stood between Andrade and Lawless, all three of them using

Grant, Beckett, Rafe, and Tate as wind blocks. "I'm trying to sleep."

"Jesus Christ." Grant bounced from foot to foot, trying to stay warm. "Don't stand still, boys, or your ass cheeks'll freeze together."

"That ain't all that'll freeze together," Lawless offered.

A murmur of movement rippled close to them. Someone nudged their way to the front of the crowd. Grant glanced that direction just as Bridgette stepped up beside him. She wore a winter-white wool trench over the barely there midnight-blue dress she'd had on at the pre-party, and slipped her arm through Grant's, snuggling up beside him.

"What are you doing here?" he asked. She hadn't been invited to the lighting, only the parties before and after as Grant's arm candy. "How'd you get in?"

"I used to date the security guy." She beamed up at him with pearly whites that made her coat look positively dingy. Her bright blue eyes danced with clandestine thrill.

In the two hours since he'd picked her up at her apartment, Bridgette had tried three times to convince him to spend the night with her. Yet all Grant could think about was Faith. Faith and what she was doing with her Christmas Eve day without the ice-sculpting contest on her agenda. Faith and all the texts she hadn't returned. Faith and his calls she hadn't taken.

He knew how to read the message she was sending loud and clear. He just wasn't used to being on the receiving end of it. And now that he was back in the middle of this hot mess he called a life, everything he'd found cute or quirky about Faith to begin with were the very things he loved about her now. Missed about her now.

And he didn't know what the hell to do about it.

Thankfully, the ceremony ended within ten minutes. Grant grabbed a private limo ride to the reception with Bridgette and spent the ten-minute drive repeating what he'd already told her earlier in the evening. But this time, he wasn't as nice about it. Bridgette pushed from the limo livid and strode past Donovan and Savage, who were waiting for him at the curb.

When Grant stood from the car to tip the driver, Rafe said, "What the hell did you do to ruin that sure thing?"

"Go find your coeds." Grant pushed his billfold back into his pants pocket and wandered their direction. He was already exhausted and it was only eight o'clock. "I'll keep the hall monitor in check."

Rafe pounded Grant's fist. "I owe you."

"Grow up," Tate yelled at Rafe's back, which he ignored.

Grant and Tate joined the reception, neither interested in being there. They spent half an hour talking about Grant's shoulder, the team, and the games Grant missed while he was in Holly. Which only reminded him of that ache in the pit of his stomach and made him glance at his phone again.

Still nothing. And God help him, all he could think about was her walking away, with her *"Safe travels, Grant Saber"* ringing in his head.

Tonight, the words felt more like a permanent good-bye than a see you later.

"Who is she?" Tate's question pulled Grant's gaze from his drink. Tate had his shoulder against a pillar, his eyes on Grant.

"Who is who?"

"The chick? The one who's not texting you back. The one who's making you wish you were somewhere else?"

"What makes you think it's a chick? Maybe I'm just sick and tired of this monkey-suit-smile-for-the-camera shit. Maybe I'm thinking about negotiating my next contract differently next time around."

"Because otherwise you'd have done Bridgette in the bathroom at the pre-party already and be looking for another empty closet somewhere in here. Or, if you'd already tired of Bridgette after one ride, you'd be prowling with Savage." Tate smiled, but it wasn't happy, and it wasn't smug. It was sad. "And, because I've been there. Not all that long ago. I recognize the signs."

*Ah shit.* Grant had forgotten about Tate's divorce. "Hey, man, I'm sorry."

"No, I'm sorry. It sucks. And I'm here to tell you, if you love her, it doesn't get any better."

Grant downed half his drink, wincing at the burn. "Just what I needed to hear tonight."

Did he love her? Grant had never been in love. He knew he was crazy about her. Certainly didn't want to think about the coming weeks and months without talking to her, seeing her, touching her.

But *love*?

"God, I'm tired." He rubbed his eyes. "I just want to go home."

No. Not home. He wanted to go to Faith.

He wanted to *go home to Faith*.

Home and Faith.

Yes.

They fit.

But, still... Was that love? And did it matter?

"If you're this tied up over her, why didn't you bring her with you?" Tate asked. "I mean, I don't blame you. That dumbass right there"—he lifted his beer toward Rafe where he was chatting up two beautiful women—"is enough reason."

Grant glanced at Rafe, then back at Tate, confused. "What?"

"The chick you're twisted over. Why didn't you just bring her with you? You could have made it a mini Christmas vacation."

He opened his mouth to answer, but every excuse he pulled up fell flat—she didn't have any family to stay in Holly for. She'd given up on judging the contest. The hardware store was closed Christmas Day.

*Why didn't I just bring her?*

A sick feeling spread across the floor of his stomach. To push it away, Grant blew Tate off. "What kind of question is that? Who'd want to come to one of these things? They're boring as shit. I don't even want to come."

"You're not serious. Dude, this is an exclusive event with the fucking president of the United States, not to mention a block-buster country music mogul. I know the whole celebrity thing doesn't do anything for you, but that doesn't mean it wouldn't do anything for *her*."

He thought of Faith's reaction to the news of his obligation. *"That's an opportunity most people will go their whole lives without ever experiencing."*

That icky feeling in his gut rose through his chest.

"Chicks *dig* this shit." Tate gestured around the room, where everyone was talking and laughing with others. "Everyone digs this shit. Well, except losers like us."

Grant was a loser, all right.

A major loser.

In fact, he was pretty sure he'd lost the best thing he'd ever found.

He replayed his last fifteen minutes with Faith over in his head again and again. *"Safe travels, Grant Saber."*

"Grant?"

A woman's smooth voice tugged him into the present, and he looked into the eyes of a woman he'd hooked up with a few months back. Kim? Kelly? Kris? Kira? Something with a K. She was so his type—so urban, so sleek, so perfect, so superficial. And he didn't even remember anything about their time in bed, just that he'd slept with her. He knew without any doubt he'd remember every minute with Faith.

"Hey," she said, smiling. "Haven't seen you in a while."

"Oh yeah," Tate said with a lift of the brows as he brought

his drink to his mouth. "I forgot who I was talking to. That's a good reason not to bring her."

Everything inside him pushed back. No. He didn't want to go back to that life. He'd touched something real, and nothing else would ever measure up.

He turned and shoved his drink into Tate's hand. "All yours. I'm done."

"What? Grant—" He pushed both drinks into one hand and grabbed Grant's arm. "You can't just walk out. The big wigs aren't even here yet."

"Then they're going to miss out, aren't they? I've met my obligations, and they weren't one of them." Grant jerked from Tate's grasp and threaded his way through the crowded room toward the exit and the limos waiting beyond.

FAITH PULLED the last package of drill bits from the last box of inventory that had once filled the shelves of her basement, and hung it on the designated hook. Releasing a sigh, she rested her hands on the top of the step stool, surveying the shelves around her for organizing opportunities. But she already knew there were none to be found—she'd organized every shelf in the store, top to bottom, end to end over the last thirty hours since she'd said good-bye to Grant.

She'd only taken a break to watch the tree-lighting ceremony—and boy had that been a mistake. Her mind replayed the sight Faith was sure she'd never forget, of Bridgette Ferreira cutting through the crowd and sliding right into place at Grant's side, smiling up at him like an adoring Barbie doll.

Her stomach dropped to her feet again with the force of a ninety-degree roller-coaster plunge. Faith's core muscles tightened to protect her against the inevitable pain. "He certainly didn't waste any time picking up where he left off."

God, she was so gullible.

So many emotions roiled inside her, they made her dizzy. She had to find something to keep her mind occupied, or she was sure she'd drive herself insane.

Faith climbed down the short ladder and snapped it closed. The metal clap echoed through the empty store. Not a soul had come through the front door in hours. Everyone in town and about a thousand other visitors were all at the festival.

And just like that, the ice-carving contest, her dad, and Natalie joined Grant in her uncomfortable thoughts. She wondered if Charlie Dumphies had won for the fourth year in a row. Wondered if anyone had missed her. And whether or not Natalie had gotten the validation she'd been looking for out of her role in the event.

Faith might never get the answers to those questions, but she had learned one important thing—she didn't need the festival the way she'd thought. She'd also learned she now didn't have anything to do to keep everyone out of her head. She hung the ladder on a hook in the back, closed her eyes, and exhaled. "It can only get better, right?"

Even if that were true, it didn't help her now. Now she just had to find a way to get through it. She turned to face the store and all its empty aisles, cleaned and straightened to perfection.

"There certainly isn't anything left to do here." Her gaze stopped on the front doors. "And I won't be making one damn sale today." A wave of anxious misery snaked through her, and she pressed a hand to her forehead as thoughts of failure, of losing the store, of going bankrupt swam in her head. "What now, Faith? What the hell are you going to do now?"

This was when those lightning strikes of anger usually came. The ones that prompted her to yell at her father for leaving her. After which she always melted into tears.

But she was just too exhausted for that kind of emotional

dump. And this place was too empty, too hollow to stay in tonight alone.

She took a few deep breaths to ease the sting of tears and did the only thing she could do. The only thing she knew how to do. The only thing that had worked for her in the past. She pulled on her jacket, collected all the notes relating to her last-ditch effort to save the store, grabbed a pencil, a notepad, the laptop, and headed into the freezing night.

While her store had been empty, Holly itself was alive with tourists and locals spilling out of the festival and strolling along the flashy streets.

In contrast, Faith traversed the adorable block in a mere ninety seconds and ducked into the warmth of Yuletide Spirits. The pub was as packed as she'd expected. Every seat at the bar was taken. Most of the tables were occupied. Quite a few people were milling among friends.

Faith caught sight of an empty one-person table in the corner, then sidestepped toward the bar and waved at Kelly.

"Hey, girl," Kelly said. "What's up?"

"Is it okay if I take the one-top in the corner for about an hour? I needed to get out of the store."

Someone yelled for service at the other end of the bar, and Kelly shot the man a glare that would have taken him off at the knees if he weren't already plastered.

When Kelly turned back to Faith, she said, "As long as you don't do *that*"—she tipped her head toward the offender—"you can have the table all night."

"Thanks." Faith pulled a twenty-dollar bill from her pocket and laid it on the bar. "Give me whatever drink has the most alcohol and cover it with enough sugar that I won't even know it's there."

Kelly pulled a glass from a shelf, set it on a rubber mat, and started mixing the drink. "That kind of day for you too, huh?"

"I need to find complete and total detachment. Fast."

"This will do it." Kelly lifted the finished drink, saluting Faith. "Here's to a quick end to Christmas Eve."

Faith pushed the twenty forward, sad that a day she'd always loved now caused her so much pain. Even sadder that she'd thought she'd found someone special to share it with only to be heartbroken.

She wove through the crowd, claimed her table, and did her best to lose herself in the combination of luscious alcohol and these strange new online business opportunities.

The alcohol shaved off an edge of stress, the crowd helped her shake the loneliness, and the ideas Grant had sketched out based on Taylor's experience were, well, pretty amazing. Simple, yet powerful. And he'd tiered the startup, adding in ways Faith could learn how to produce the most effective videos, write the most interesting blogs, find the best sponsorships, set up the most profitable affiliate links...

"Shit," she murmured, looking over his smooth, slanted male handwriting. "This is so...doable."

Turning to Taylor's pages, Faith looked at the different numbers again to see where her friend's profits came from. Compared that to Grant's plan. And, hell, even if Faith consistently made ten percent of what Taylor did, it would help make ends meet. Thirty percent and she'd be secure, with the extra cash she needed to expand the business in ways that would bring in more sales, more contracts, more customers. Fifty percent and she'd be *floating*. She'd already made a couple thousand dollars in affiliate income on her single Christmas Fantasia Light Show video.

Excitement sparked hope. Hope lifted her mood. Maybe she'd get out from under this black cloud after all.

At least financially. Personally...that was another story.

"I've been looking all over for you."

Between the time the male voice touched her ears and the time she looked into the man's eyes, Faith realized it was Grant.

Her stomach fluttered into her throat, but a protective barrier closed around her heart.

"What...?" They'd been broadcasting the Christmas tree lighting live from DC just a few hours ago. He should be at some party with all those famous people she'd seen in the crowd. Or at his place doing Bridgette. Faith glanced over him. "Is that...a tux?"

"Yeah. Long story. Can we talk? Maybe back at the store where it's quiet?"

Her gut clenched around a tug of war between her heart and her gut. *Stand up for yourself, Faith. No one else will do it for you.*

"No. I came here to get away from the store."

He sighed, looked around. "Okay."

He disappeared into the crowd, giving Faith time to breathe. Time to process his sudden return. She hadn't known whether he would be coming back to town or not. And she'd made peace with their good-bye.

But now her guts were churning again. Her heart aching again. She couldn't do this. She shouldn't have to do this.

And the fact was...she *didn't* have to do this.

Faith pushed all her papers into a pile and grabbed the laptop. But before she could stand, he was back with a chair. He dropped it opposite her booth seat and gently pulled her things from her arms, setting them on the table.

"I'm in the middle of something here." *Hold on to the anger. Hold on to the anger.* If she didn't, she'd cave. "The world doesn't revolve around you, superstar."

He laughed. It was a tired, you-are-so-freaking-adorable laugh. "Man, I missed you." He leaned forward and took her hands. "That had to be the longest thirty-six hours of my ever-loving life."

"Stop, Grant." She pulled her hands back. "Look, I understand you have a life somewhere else. But I'm not going to be just another woman in another port you can drop in on anytime it suits you."

"Whoa..." He leaned forward and braced his forearms on his thighs. "Faith, where did that come from?"

"I watched the event on television. Did you *want* me to see you with her? Was it some bizarre game to boost your ego?" She couldn't do this. She was going to snap. "I said good-bye. And I meant it."

"I know. And, like an idiot, I didn't realize that until just a few hours ago."

God, she was tired—tired of fighting, tired of losing, tired of hurting. "She pressed her elbow to the table and dropped her head into her hand, trying to get rid of the tears before they fell. "Grant, don't," she begged. "It was so good. I don't want it to end like this."

His big hand cupped her cheek. He leaned close, his voice a heavy, urgent rasp. "I don't want it to end at all."

She rolled her eyes and sat back. "I already told you—"

"I don't want anyone but you. I didn't ask Bridgette to the event. You can ask my agent—he set Bridgette up as my date for the parties before and after because he didn't know I was seeing you. She wasn't supposed to be there. That's why she showed up at the very end and was only there for a few minutes." His explanation—even if it wasn't true, though she was starting to think it might be, because why would he have come all this way when he had Bridgette willing to bang him in DC?—softened the edge off her hurt and anger.

And they sat there a long moment, staring at each other, his eyes begging.

"I was waiting for the president to get to the reception," he finally said, "so I could take a damn picture with him and go home, when I realized that while I was saying good-bye to you for the day, you were saying good-bye to me for good."

He suddenly seemed vulnerable in a way she'd never imagined this big strong hockey player could.

Her throat thickened with emotion, but there was still too much gray space between truth and fiction. "Seemed like the right time. It was inevitable, and I didn't see the point in dragging it out."

"Thing is…" He leaned forward again and collected one of her hands between his. Faith didn't pull it away, but she didn't engage either. And it was excruciatingly difficult. "I don't see it as inevitable. A few days ago, I wanted to ask if you'd think about continuing to see me."

Faith's heart tripped, and her mind scanned backward. She hadn't seen any sign of that.

"But, man, that's no small thing in my world. And you've had so much to deal with, I didn't want to put another pressure on your shoulders."

Disbelief narrowed Faith's eyes. "I'm not your type. I'm not even *close* to your type."

He exhaled, long and slow, then thought a minute. "Okay," he finally said, "I'm going to talk fast, because I know you're not going to listen for long. You're right, you're not my type. Which is exactly why I can't shake you. Why it felt like I was gone a month when I was only gone a day. Why I fell so damn hard for you. And why I can't even *think* about another woman."

A current traveled through her chest. She didn't know if it was excitement, fear, or anger, but she pushed her chair back. She needed space—to think, to breathe.

"The women I've seen over the past few years have all been just like Bridgette," he went on. "They don't care about anyone or anything but themselves and what they want. They care about their looks, their image, and their money. I slept with them because neither of us was looking for anything more than sex. They were easy to come by and easy to let go. But you were different from the start."

Faith's heart was beating so fast, she pressed her hand to her chest. "Grant—"

"When I was in DC after being here for two weeks, I could barely stand it. Everyone felt plastic. Everything felt scripted. And all I wanted to do was come home. Only I didn't want to come back here for Holly, or even my family. I wanted to come back for *you,* Faith. I wanted to come back because..." He released a breath, looked away, then looked back, and that vulnerability had returned. The one that twisted her heart. "I came back because *you* feel like home to me. And I don't want to let that go. I don't want to let *you* go."

All Faith's breath rushed out on a soft sound of shock. "But...you have to go back. Your life is there. Mine is here. I have to figure out the store..." She pressed a hand to her face. Dropped back in the chair. And in her mind's eye, her life spun like a cyclone. "I... You... *How?*"

He pressed an elbow to the table and rested his forehead against his fingers. "This is why I didn't bring it up before I left. I don't have an easy answer. The regular season doesn't end until mid-April. If we go into the playoffs, it won't end until June. We get the summer off—mostly—and training camps start up in September."

He leaned forward and slid his hands up her thighs until he took hers again. "I haven't thought through the details yet. I only know that I've been with enough women to know when I've found someone different, someone special, someone worth holding on to. And I want that with you, Faith. I want to at least try to make this work."

His pretty eyes brightened with hope. So much hope. So much honesty. Her dad had always said she was a good judge of character. If he were here, he would tell her that all she could do was base her decision on what she knew of Grant firsthand, not gossip or hearsay. He'd tell Faith to trust her gut and follow her heart.

And Faith's mind was spinning, trying to find a way to make it feasible. She didn't realize how long she'd been lost in thought until Grant shrugged one shoulder and dropped his gaze. "If that's not what you want, or it's too soon—"

Faith reached for his face, cupped his jaw, and lifted his gaze to hers. "It's what I want," she said breathlessly. "But, I'm not gonna lie, it scares the hell out of me."

Relief washed over his features, and a smile brightened his face. The sight of the clouds clearing from his expression brought joy to Faith's heart. She leaned in and kissed him. And with her lips against his, she knew—this was right. This was where she belonged now. It was the right time to take this risk.

When she pulled back, he brushed hair off her face. "I was thinking about it a lot on the way home. My lifestyle isn't great. I travel—*a lot*. But the owner bought the team a new plane last year, one that's more efficient and faster and seats almost a hundred people. That means I'm usually home the same night I play. And if we've got back-to-back games where we'll be gone awhile, the owner lets the guys bring their girlfriends or wives. The team would cover your expenses on those trips like they cover mine—hotel, food."

"Wait, what...?" Streaks of heat coursed through Faith's chest. Panic? Fear? Excitement? God, she wasn't sure. "I don't understand..."

He reached out and tucked a strand of her hair behind her ear. His eyes were soft and drenched with affection. He looked at her in a way no one had looked at her since high school.

"I waited too long to tell you how I felt a couple of days ago, and I almost lost you. I'm not going to risk that again. You can always say no, but I won't always have the opportunity to offer. I'd really like you to consider moving to DC with me."

"Oh my God." Her world tipped on its axis. She put a hand over her hammering heart.

He lifted his hands as if that would stop the barrage of

thoughts and emotion that poured through her. "I know it's a lot to ask, and if you're not sure about us, we can find you your own place. But, man, I *really* love the idea of coming home to you after a long day on the ice, and that is something I *never* thought I'd say. My place is way too big for one person, so you'd have plenty of your own space. And yeah, it pretty much looks like a bachelor pad, but I could deal with some changes." He grinned a little. "You know, small ones."

That made her laugh, but her lungs felt way too small, and she couldn't seem to get enough air.

"There's real possibility in Taylor's business model for you, and you can blog and tape videos from anywhere. You've already been thinking about making Joe manager, which would allow you to concentrate on this new business plan. And, baby, I would set you up one *killer* studio in the extra bedroom. I'm talkin' professional-grade equipment."

She laughed. "Sounds like a bribe."

"Call it what you want. And"—he winced—"don't get pissed, but I was so excited about the possibilities for this new venture that on the way home, I called another player who's dating one of the anchors on a local morning show, and asked him to pitch the idea of a weekly Fix-It segment—"

"*What?*"

His wince transitioned into a grimace. "You don't have to do it. It's just in the idea phase—"

"Oh my God." She squeezed his hands. "That's amazing. This is just all so—"

"Overwhelming. I know. I'm sorry. It sounds like I'm going to get called back in the next day or two, and I want you to know everything before I have to leave. You don't have to make any decisions until you're ready." He threaded their fingers. "We'll just have to have phone sex."

That made Faith burst out laughing and allowed her to take a full deep breath.

"You could fly from New York to Ashville with just one connection," Grant continued. "It's about three hours, and I've got a ton of frequent-flier miles you could use. You could come here once a month if you want, more often if you need to. When I'm not playing or training, I could come with you, but realistically, that won't be until June, which is why I'm asking about you moving in with me and not offering to move here for you."

"The fact that you even thought about it says everything." She put a hand to her temple. "You're making my head spin."

He grinned. "Tell me about it." But then he just kept talking, his enthusiasm growing. "DC is such a cool place to live. God, there's so much to show you. There's always something to do. And I think you'd really enjoy the team. They're no different from the guys you deal with in your store every day, and I know you'd be a welcome change to some of the high-maintenance women the other guys have in their lives. There's a lot of laughter, bitching, practical jokes, and a whole hell of a lot of meals and hanging out together. We're sort of one big ugly family, for better or worse."

Faith's nose stung with encroaching tears. But these were happy tears. "That sounds..." *Warm, joyous, fun...* She laughed. "Amazing."

His brows shot up, and his eyes took on that stunned glaze. "Yeah?"

She stroked his face. "And scary and unnerving, but yeah." She kissed him and rested her forehead against his. "If you're sure you want me around that much, I'm sure I'm ready to give it a try."

"No way." He pulled back, eyes wide. "Really?"

She laughed. "Why are you so surprised?"

"Well... It's... Because..." He regrouped. "Honestly, I didn't think you'd leave the store. And I didn't think you'd leave Holly. This is your home."

She curled her fingers into Grant's collar. "My dad always said, home is only home because the people you love are there." She scraped her bottom lip between her teeth, the realization that she had fallen so hard for this man so quickly making her nerves tighten and shiver. "So wherever you are, I guess that's going to be my home from now on."

He cupped her face, scanning every inch while more emotions flashed through his eyes. Warm, real emotions that made Faith feel like the most beautiful, most wanted woman in the world.

"Have I told you lately," he asked, "how amazing you are?"

"I doubt a girl could get tired of hearing something like that."

He pulled her into his lap and wrapped his arms around her waist. "You, Faith Nicholas, are a-freaking-mazing. And if you're willing to put up with my bullshit during the season, I am willing to indulge your every desire off-season." He grinned. "And every night, on *or* off season. I am so crazy about you, I can't even put it into words."

He kissed her again, and that light-headed sensation returned, making Faith dizzy with happiness. She opened to him for a long, deep kiss filled with emotion. And when she pulled back, she stroked his cheek. "What do you say we close this deal...in my room?"

Grant laughed and pulled her against him, holding her tight. "Baby," he murmured in her ear, "I'd say this is going to be one *very* merry Christmas."

# EPILOGUE

O*ne week later*

"Oh my God, it's packed." Faith stood just inside the door to Yuletide Spirits, where the pub was filled with cheerful celebrants.

After spending the last week in Washington, DC—including nights with her face all but pressed up against the glass of the Verizon stadium, watching Grant play three games between Christmas and New Year—she should be used to crowds. She just wasn't used to them in Holly.

Grant squeezed in behind her, letting the door close on the blustery night outside, and slipped his arms around her waist, pressing his body to hers. He was warm and strong, and he filled Faith with the kind of joy no words could describe.

He lowered his head and spoke into her ear. "We could always ring in the new year at your place."

She grinned, turned her head, and kissed him. "Oh, that's definitely going to happen. Right after we stop by and say hi to Taylor and drop off Caleb's jersey."

"You want to give him that tonight?" Grant asked. "He'll never get to sleep."

Faith laughed. Grant had all the Rough Riders sign a jersey for Caleb, and he was right—Caleb would be so excited, sleep might be tough. But she said, "He'll sleep *in* it. And we only have"—she glanced at the screen where the New Year's countdown continued—"eight minutes until we can go do that."

He tightened his arms and pressed his face to her neck. His nose was cold, but his lips were warm. "Eight minutes never felt like such an eternity."

Happiness spread across her face in a smile that made her cheeks ache. Anticipation for the future bubbled in her chest like the champagne flowing at the bar.

Grant released her to remove her jacket just as Patrick and his girlfriend, Jennifer, pushed their way through the crowd. Faith had met them both during Christmas dinner at the Saber house—Jennifer for the first time, Patrick for the first time in a decade—and was surprised to find she enjoyed both Grant's brother and his choice in women.

"Hey," Jennifer said, her eyes alight with excitement.

"Hi." Faith hugged Jennifer and said hello to Patrick over his girlfriend's shoulder. "This place is crazy. How long have you been here?"

Jennifer pulled back. "Right? Only half an hour, but I think my hearing's already damaged."

Grant cupped a hand around one ear and leaned forward. "What?"

Laughing, Jennifer slapped his arm.

The crowd parted as more people came through.

"Mom?" Grant said, his voice lifting with surprise. "Dad? What the heck...?"

When Jennifer stepped aside, Faith saw Grant's parents approaching. Hazel looked happy, maybe even a little tipsy. Martin didn't look exactly thrilled to be there, but he was, which meant he was making an effort. It was a first step.

"What are you two even doing awake at this hour?" Grant asked.

"We knew you'd come straight here from the airport." His mother came directly to Faith and took her hands. Her eyes shone with excitement. "And I couldn't wait until tomorrow to hear about it. So? How did it go?"

Faith's heart softened, and she squeezed Hazel's hands. For all the pain his parents had caused Grant, they were sincerely trying to make amends now. They had already scheduled trips to see two of Grant's games in the coming months and planned to stay a few extra days in the city so Grant could show them around. Patrick and Jennifer had also scheduled trips into DC for visits and games. And while it might take some time for Grant's older brother, Shawn, to come around, things were definitely headed in the right direction.

"Oh my gosh," Faith told Hazel. "It was amazing. Really amazing. Wait until you see Grant's apartment. The view—ridiculous. And everywhere he goes, someone asks for his autograph or a picture. Watching him play...just, wow. I have no words. You will be *so proud*."

Hazel smiled at Grant. "I'm looking forward to it." She returned her gaze to Faith. "And the segment taping? How did it go?"

"*So* good." She rolled her eyes as another gush of pleasure rolled through. "I still can't believe how good."

"She's a natural." Grant's voice came from behind her just before his hands closed on her shoulders and slid down her arms. He leaned in and kissed her head. "And she looks gorgeous on camera."

Hazel laughed. "I have no doubt."

"When will you start taping shows?" Martin asked, stepping into the conversation.

Before Faith could answer, Kelly climbed onto the bar and

shouted, "Grab your drinks and your significant others, everyone. We've got a minute until the New Year kicks in."

Patrick dragged Jennifer to his side, Grant's father wrapped his arm around Hazel's shoulders, and Grant tucked Faith into their own little corner and pulled her close.

Faith relaxed into his arms and smiled up at him. "Do you want to grab a drink before the ball falls?"

"Nope." He lifted a hand to tuck a strand of hair behind her ear. "My mouth is going to be busy in other ways far more pleasant than drinking."

God, her chest ached with the pressure of the love filling her. "You're amazing. I have no words to tell you how incredible the last two weeks have been for me."

Grant's gaze rested on hers, soft and sweet with all the love he returned. "I have to tell you, baby, there was nothing like playing and winning at my home rink, knowing you were right there watching. Absolutely nothing more fulfilling or settling or thrilling than coming out of that locker room after the game to find you there, this gorgeous smile on your face." He shook his head. "I never knew I could love like this, and I know everything has happened cyclone fast, but I can't imagine ever being without you."

She leaned into him, tilted her face up, and slid her hand around the back of his neck. "You'll never need to. I'm not going anywhere."

Grant lowered his forehead to hers as the crowd started the countdown. But neither Grant nor Faith were interested in looking at anything but each other as the count reached one and he took her face in both hands.

Cheers and horns and bells filled the pub. But before Grant kissed her, with his lips a breath away, Faith said, "I love you, Grant Saber."

He paused. "And I love you, Faith Nicholas."

They were both smiling when they kissed, surrounded by the rowdy bar.

His lips were warm, his kiss soft and filled with emotion. Everything in Faith's world righted and filled. And when she pulled back, Faith discovered romantic love wasn't the only love destined to enter their lives in the New Year.

Hazel and Martin asked them over for breakfast the next morning. Patrick and Jennifer asked them to go out to dinner the following night. Grant had already promised Caleb a guys-only movie day so Faith could check in on the store and grab some quality time with Taylor to talk business.

Their short time back in Holly before they returned to DC, Grant's hectic schedule, and Faith's new career venture was packed. But it was packed with good things.

After making dates for the following day, Grant wrapped an arm at her waist and whispered, "Ready to take this celebration to a private location?" Faith knew she'd found that kind of love. The kind that fulfilled and supported and gave her a new perspective on life. A perspective that allowed her to stretch to become who she was meant to be.

She leaned her head back against Grant's shoulder, looked him in the eye, and said, "My dad would have really loved you."

A moment of confusion passed before he smiled, kissed her temple, and squeezed her tight. "And I would have loved your dad, because he created the most beautiful woman in the world —inside and out."

She turned in Grant's arms and linked her hands at the back of his neck. "Let's get this year started off right."

On their way toward the door, they said a few good-byes and stepped outside, where Holly's quiet, snowy night wrapped them in the familiar arms of what the town had always offered, those timeless gifts of the Christmas season three hundred and sixty-five days a year: hope, love, and the promise of miracles.

# ABOUT THE AUTHOR

Skye Jordan is the *New York Times* and *USA Today* bestselling author of more than thirty novels.

When she's not writing, Skye loves to learn new things and enjoys staying active, so you're just as likely to find her in the ceramics studio as out rowing on the nearest lake or river.

She and her husband have two beautiful daughters and live in Oregon.

**Connect with Skye online**

**Amazon | Instagram | Facebook | Website | Newsletter | Reader Group | Tiktok**

## ALSO BY SKYE JORDAN

ROUGH RIDERS HOCKEY SERIES

Quick Trick

Hot Puck

Dirty Score

Wild Zone

PHOENIX RISING

Hot Blooded

Shadow Warrior

Hell Hath no Fury

Wicked Wrath

FORGED IN FIRE

Flashpoint

Smoke and Mirrors

Playing with Fire

WILDFIRE LAKE SERIES

In Too Deep

Going Under

Swept Away

NASHVILLE HEAT

So Wright

Damn Wright

Must be Wright

MANHUNTERS SERIES

Grave Secrets

No Remorse

Deadly Truths (Coming Soon)

RENEGADES SERIES

Reckless

Rebel

Ricochet

Rumor

Relentless

Rendezvous

Riptide

Rapture

Risk

Ruin

Rescue (Coming Soon)

Roulette (Coming Soon)

QUICK & DIRTY COLLECTION:

Dirtiest Little Secret

WILDWOOD SERIES:

Forbidden Fling

Wild Kisses

COVERT AFFAIRS SERIES

Intimate Enemies

First Temptation

Sinful Deception

Printed in Great Britain
by Amazon